GRAVE MISTAK
Grave Diggers Se1
- Book 3 -

by
Chris Fritschi

DISCLAIMER

This is a work of fiction. Names, characters, businesses, places, events and incidents are either the products of the author's imagination or used in a fictitious manner. Any resemblance to actual persons, living or dead, or actual events is purely coincidental.

Grave Mistakes
by
Chris Fritschi

V3

ISBN:
ISBN-13:

Click or visit
chrisfritschi.com

To Karen. Your encouragement, honesty and belief in me fuel my spirit.

ACKNOWLEDGMENTS

The pages of his book are the result of all the people who gave their input, guidance, and knowledge. Thank you all.

A special thanks to all of you, you know who you are, for the encouragement and finger wagging that kept me on my toes through the development of this book. The critical, but honest, input from my beta-readers Cinnamon, Becka, Samantha, Lauren. You guys make me look good.

Enough can't be said for my wife who spent endless hours listening to me brain-dump over this book. Her patience and support never flagged.

1

NOTHING IS FREE

The slide snapped forward on the pistol's lovingly oiled rails with a satisfying *clack*.

"Stop screwing around with that," said Lubbock. "You're making me nervous."

Shelp eyed his partner disapprovingly and holstered his pistol.

Arrayed on the desk, in front of them, were feeds from multiple security cameras. The staff had gone home hours ago leaving the security guards to their nightly vigil of watching empty corridors and locked doors.

Lubbock took another bite out of his hotdog before swallowing the previous bite. "You gotta calm down with that ninja, gunslinger act."

"That," said Shelp critically, pointing to a soggy lump of half chewed food rolling down Lubbock's shirt. "That, right there is why I'm here. This complex is a critical communications hub responsible for transmitting vital and classified information and you treat it like it's a kitchen. They reassigned me to this post because I can be depended to defend this site from hostile elements."

The forward momentum of the lump of food wasn't enough to get over the swell of Lubbock's belly and it stopped against a button. Lubbock looked at it for a moment, deciding it's fate. "Hostile elements?" said Lubbock as he flicked the food off his shirt. "Who? We're not at war with anyone. This is South America, not a war zone."

"It's complacency like yours that makes America a sitting duck to attack," said Shelp. "Unlike you, I've honed my awareness. There's threats everywhere."

"Like that janitor you almost shot?" said Lubbock. "That's what got you reassigned."

"Janitor. Right. I got reassigned to cover-up what's going on there," said Shelp with an edge in his voice. "Why was the janitor there *after* the building was closed? Why did he run?"

"You shot at him," said Lubbock.

"*That* was an accidental discharge," growled Shelp.

"Discharge is right," Lubbock chuckled wetly through his mouth of food. "You're lucky they didn't discharge you to jail."

"I'm going to do a patrol," said Shelp, abruptly standing.

"What?" said Lubbock. "Aw, come on. We already did our scheduled patrol and clock out in a few minutes."

Shelp unlocked the dull, grey cabinet behind them and took out a bull-pup assault rifle. Lubbock's eyes widened with alarm as Shelp inspected the magazine.

"Whoa, hang on," protested Lubbock. "We don't touch those unless there's an armed break in."

Shelp slapped the loaded magazine into the assault rifle. "How do you know someone's not breaking in right now?" he said. "I'm not waiting until it's too late to find out."

Shelp picked up the master key-card and disappeared around the corner leaving a worried Lubbock looking at the clock.

"That psycho's gonna make me late getting home."

Dim grey-blue light outlined row upon row of steel monoliths brooding in the shadows as banks of tiny, green and orange status lights blinked across their faces. The temperature hung at a constant forty three degrees as each server pumped terabytes of data through miles of cables. Collectively, the low hum of their cooling fans sounded like a distant roar as they inhaled the cold air across their processors.

Sergeant Major Jack Tate and Sergeant Tyler Rosse stood next to the exit door as silent sentinels, ignoring their shivering as they stared intently at a pair of legs sticking out, below a distant server.

The legs disappeared inside the eviscerated belly of the server, occasionally shifting as their owner struggled for a comfortable position. Sergeant Bret Monkhouse's slim build didn't provide much padding against the unforgiving metal struts of the server's shell making him wince as he propped his elbow on the hard angles. Using his free hand he traced a yellow data cable through a confusing knot of identical cables leading beyond his view.

"Wesson, I'm trying another lead," grunted Monkhouse into his radio mike as he struggled to fasten a clip to the yellow cable.

"Standing by," crackled Wesson's voice in his earpiece.

A narrow bundle of wires ran from the clip into a small, flat display about the size of a pack of cards.

Far away, Sergeant Lori Wesson sat transfixed at a desk, her face lit by the blue-white static on the monitor in front of her. Her pale green eyes searched the screen until bold characters began marching across the bottom of the screen. "I got it," she said.

"Look for the SUID," said Monkhouse, "and give me the code that follow it.

Wesson scanned her finger over the screen, slowly filling with a jumble of meaningless symbols, numbers and letters. "Found it! SUID. Five, five, charlie, zero."

Monkhouse swore under his breath. "Are you sure that's a zero and not the letter O, like oscar. The Specified Unique Identification has to be..."

"I know the difference," Wesson cut in.

"All right. All right," said Monkhouse as he took the clip off the data cable. "That leaves one cable left."

"Then that's got to be it," said Wesson, encouraged.

"If this is the right server," said Monkhouse.

Wesson frowned at her watch. The simple, but durable device indifferently counted down the minutes. "We're running out of time."

Monkhouse ignored her as he stretched to put the clip on another data cable. "It's not like they put big signs on them saying, 'tap this line'," he said. He was feeling the effects of the cold and contortions he performed to access the data interface. His hands were tired and his fingers beginning to cramp.

Tate's eyes shifted to the door, in alarm, as his ears picked up the distant sound of bootsteps in the hallway.

At the end of the hallway, Shelp came around the corner and stopped at the first door. Automated lights came on, illuminating several plain doors lining the hall. Shelp slung his assault rifle over his shoulder as he fished his key card out of his pocket and held it up to the door's security sensor. With a chirp the sensor glowed green and the guard heard the electronic lock slide open.

With one smooth movement he swept the assault rifle up, bracing the stock against his shoulder. He quickly turned the doorknob and pushed the door open to the darkened room. He thumbed the switch to the under-barrel flashlight mounted to his gun, stabbing the darkness with a brilliant stark-white beam that made him squint. Looking down the barrel of his rifle, he panned the room until he was satisfied there were no intruders.

Down the hallway Tate heard the door close and the sound of the guards boots walking to the next door. Rosse nodded grimly acknowledging he heard it too and shrugged his broad shoulders prompting Tate for direction.

"Monkhouse," whispered Tate into his radio. "We have to abort."

"Are you kidding?" said Monkhouse. "I'm just getting the sensor on the last cable."

"We can't abort," hissed Rosse.

"Rosse is right," said Wesson over the radio. The electronic shielding of the building walls made it hard to hear her radio signal, but there was no mistaking the tension in her voice. "This is the only shot we have."

Outside, Tate heard another chirp as the guard unlocked the next door.

"Win or lose, this is the last one, Monkhouse," said Tate.

"All ready ahead of you, Top," said Monkhouse. "Come on, Wesson. Give me some good news."

Tate moved his mike so close to his mouth his stubble rasped against it when he spoke. "Enough chatter," he growled. "Exercise proper radio procedure."

Wesson momentarily blinked at the rebuke, but her expression changed to sharp concentration when the pixel noise of her display was broken as characters began filling the screen. She quickly found what she was looking for. "Authenticate. SUID, zero, alpha, kilo, seven, eight."

"That's it! I mean, I authenticate," said Monkhouse rolling his blue eyes at the unnecessary formalities. "I just need to plug in the tap and we're done."

Another chirp, this one much louder as the guard unlocked the next door. Tate and Rosse traded expressionless nods, neither wanting to admit the surge of adrenaline that shot through them. The sound was very close. Their door was next. Rosse glanced at the security access panel next to their door as if it was going to bite him.

Tate reached behind his back, to his belt and silently slid his tomahawk out of the sheath. Flexing his grip on the handle, the lethal weapon's gunmetal finish made it nearly invisible in the gloom. Only the naked metal of the axes razor edge could be seen softly reflecting the muted light. Even in this age of advanced technology there was a place for this weapon of noseless brutality.

Turning inside the cramped metal box of the server, Monkhouse banged into the side panel with the sound of kicking a bass drum making Rosse jump. "Quiet!" hissed Tate.

"Sorry," said Monkhouse, sarcastically. There was nothing the team could do but watch and wait, and Monkhouse's frayed nerves were making him resentful of the burden he was carrying.

Wesson stared at her watch trying to will the second-had to stop. "Less than a minute left," she said. "It's all on you."

"Yeah," said Monkhouse. "No pressure." He disconnected the clip and stuffed the small device into his pocket. From his other pocket he pulled out a small, square box, with an open ring in the top. "I'm connecting the packet splitter now." Reaching over his head he tried to clip the ring around the data cable, but his hand was shaking from fatigue and the cable was at the end of his reach. With each try the cable glanced off the ring. He needed to be closer. Monkhouse clenched his teeth to fight back the frustration and stress that had been building up to the thundering storm that wanted to explode out of him. He was chilled, tired, cramped and sore. The edges of the metal cross-frame he laid on bit into him like a bed of nails. Every time he moved he traded one part of his abused body for a new one.

Wrestling against time and the cramped space, his temper overruled his caution and he moved too sharply, pinching a grey cable under his shoulder and pulling it from its plug.

The whirring sound above his head stopped. "Oh no," groaned Monkhouse as he watched the blades of the large cooling fan stop. Immediately the green status light on the fan changed to amber.

"Oh no, what?" asked Tate.

"I just unplugged the cooling fan," explained Monkhouse.

"Big deal," said Rosse. "Tap the line and lets blow."

Monkhouse reached behind his back, groping for the disconnected cable. A second amber LED lit up on the fan's temperature sensor. "These servers generate a lot of heat and that fan's critical to keeping this one cool." His fingers dug into a tangle of cables, feeling for the loose one.

"If I don't get the fan going," said Monkhouse, "the heat sensor will hit red and an alarm will go off."

Feeling for the cable wasn't working. The servers frame rattled as Monkhouse twisted around to see what he was searching for. His eyes lit up as he saw the cable inches from where he'd been groping. Plucking the cable from the tangle of others he was about to twist around again and plug it in when a hand clamped down on his ankle making him flinch in alarm. His yelp died on his lips as he saw Tate scowling at him. Tate put his finger to his lips and pointed towards the door.

Shelp stopped at the door to the server room. With his assault rifle ready he swiped the security card. The sensor chirped and he turned the doorknob.

Rosses breath caught in his throat as he watched the doorknob turn. The door rattled, but didn't open.

In the hallway, Shelp frowned and swiped the keycard in front of the sensor again. The sensor turned green and chirped, but the door wouldn't open.

In the gloom of the server room Tate winked at Rosse who glanced at the destroyed circuity and cut wires hanging from the door's security lock panel then gave Tate a thumbs-up.

Nudging Tate with his foot, Monkhouse gestured that he'd gotten the cooling fan cable and pointed at the fan. The second to last LED blinked dark orange. Tate shook his head for Monkhouse to stay still.

Outside, the guard pulled his radio from his belt. "Base, this is Sector Echo. One of the doors won't unlock. Do you show a fault on your board? Over."

The static of Shelps radio was short lived as Lubbocks irritated voice broke in. "What are you doing?"

"It's Shelp," answered the guard stiffly. "I'm in sector ..."

"Yeah, sector echo," crackled the radio. "You gotta door that won't open. What do you want me to do about it? Mobilize a quick reaction team? Maybe come down there and shoot the lock off?"

"Base," continued Shelp. "We're responsible for the security of..."

"Give it a rest, hero," chided Lubbock. "You're running me past my shift. Get back here and write it up in your report."

Sweat matted Monkhouse's short brown hair and trickled down his face. Wiping at his stinging eyes he contorted his body to reach the plug, but was short by inches. Desperate he held the cable several inches back from the plug and for an instant it looked like he had it, but the tremble from his straining arm caused the plug to bump uselessly away from the fans connection port.

Tate looked to Rosse who signaled that the guard was still outside. Tate couldn't wait anymore. Betting everything on Monkhouse being quieter than the heat sensor alarm Tate let go of Monkhouse. Free to move, Monkhouse quickly turned his torso and slipped the plug into the cooling fan. Instantly the fan's motor whirred to life and the LED's began flicking off.

Outside, Shelp seated his radio back in its holster and frowned a last time at the door before walking down the hallway and disappearing around the corner.

"He's gone," said Rosse.

"Thirty seconds!" said Wesson.

Finally free to move, Monkhouse shuffled around sounding like boots tumbling in a clothes dryer. "This has got to be it," he said clipping the scanner ring onto a cable. Monkhouse mumbled a silent prayer to whatever divine power would listen to him.

Wesson's knuckles whitened as she gripped her chair, eyes locked on the screen of static. She dared to look away at the timer as it mercilessly killed off the remaining seconds when the screen flashed with scrolling data. "That's it!" she cried, as a large screen, behind her, came to life. "Monkhouse, you genius, you did it."

Every straining muscle in Monkhouse went limp at the same time as he basked in relief. Tate patted his leg and gave him smile.

"I think everyone in the team owes this man a case of beer," said Tate warmly. "Each. Wesson, I hope you're recording that feed. We'll watch it when we get back."

Wesson turned her chair towards the big screen hanging on the wall. An announcer grinned as he shouted into his mic only to be drowned out by the packed stadium as the fans cheered while the Los Angeles Rams came onto the field.

"Roger that," smiled Wesson.

"And no spoilers," said Rosse over the radio.

"I won't even say who wins the coin toss," chuckled Wesson.

Fulton sat in front of Wesson's desk on the sagging couch in the teams common room, staring at the TV in awe bordering on reverence. "We have TV," said Fulton dreamily to Wesson. "I'm never going to bed, again."

2

VULCAN 4

High above the Earth cold moonlight shimmered across the Black and Mediterranean seas sharply contrasting the darken void of the surrounding continents. Civilizations betrayed themselves in clusters of lights that speckled the land like splatters of molten gold. A jagged red tendril of an uncontrolled wildfire snaked across the eastern plain of Siberia. There were not enough living to fight it.

Indifferent to the breath-taking view the wide-band global SATCOM system WGS 7/1 satellite kept orbit at twenty two thousand, six hundred and eighty three miles above the Earth. Traveling at 1.9 miles a second the satellite, referred to as Vulcan 4, continued its solitary orbit as it had for several years.

A primary platform for transmitting highly classified communications, Vulcan 4 belonged to the U.S. National Reconnaissance Office; one of the "big five" United States intelligence agencies including the NSA, CIA, DARPA and a host of others.

Although the communication satellite was fully functional for another two years its diminishing fuel cells was deemed justification enough to fund, build and launch a newer, more advanced communications satellite.

As such, Vulcan 4 was sent into the junkyard zone of high earth orbit until its replacement had passed the six months of testing and everyone was confident it was working and holding orbit. Once testing was complete Vulcan 4 would be sent a command to fire its maneuvering thrusters beyond earths orbit, where it would eventually feel the tug of the suns gravity. Over time the sun would reel in Vulcan 4 until the incredible heat vaporized it.

At least that was the plan, but Vulcan 4, like many things, had been forgotten when death swept across the world in a terrifying hoard of remorseless carnage.

When it started, before anyone could comprehend the magnitude what was happening, the undead, later named Victus Mortuus (Latin for living dead), or Vix, for short, were ripping though entire populations in a feeding frenzy throughout the world.

For a while unimaginable theories and speculations grasped for a 'how' and 'why' at the origin and meaning of the Vix. Two years later the only indisputable truth was that the Vix had nearly exterminated the human race. It was believed that some countries had been entirely wiped out. That was the fate of South America. The tidal wave of undead grew in mass as it rolled across the continent.

Science had long ago proven the speed and strength of the human body when it was unfettered from the fears, doubts and limitations of the mind. The raw power and frenzied savagery of the Vix was staggering and no one person could face them unarmed.

While some cities and towns in America were overrun, others fought for their survival. People quickly realized running away only delayed a certain death. Subjugation, surrender, or negotiation didn't exist to the Vix. Only gorging on the living.

It was no surprise that some chose to horde and loot instead of taking their place alongside those risking their lives against the Vix. But that came to a sudden end when people began shooting looters on sight.

Two years later the United States had survived, but was far from unscathed. Small towns and cities across the country ceased to exist. Agriculture and industries had been crippled.

Most populations now existed in relative security within cities and towns surrounded with fortifications much like in medieval times. Outside the walls the Vix roamed and though there was talk their numbers had dwindled, at least locally, the Vix were an ever present danger.

Nobody understood how, or why, but when a person died there was a 50/50 chance they could turn into a Vix. Science could not find an answer to this riddle. Because of this a death was as feared as a dirty bomb. Just like the bombs ability to spread deadly nuclear radiation the death from a lone Vix would multiply with every victim. Each victim becoming and spawning more Vix. An entire town could be wiped out if this cascade effect wasn't stopped early enough. That wasn't speculation. It had happened multiple times.

Strict laws were enacted regarding a persons death. Those dying from disease were kept in restraints. Any fatality from unnatural causes had to be reported. Anyone who committed murder, but left the victim's skull and brain intact would receive an automatic death sentence without the possibility of appeal.

The rise of the Vix changed the world way beyond the obvious carnage of the human race. The Vix were the epicenter of a gargantuan butterfly effect working in reverse creating small, but significant ripple effects.

One of these ripples stopped the scheduled jettison of Vulcan 4 out of Earth's orbit because Derick Richards, the technician responsible for the demise of Vulcan 4 had had been eviscerated by the Vix in the middle of runway 19C of the Dulles International Airport as he hopelessly tried to flag down a taxing Boeing 7100.

The login screen for the National Reconnaissance Office held none of the colorful embellishments, or exciting images of their public web page. Other than the agency's logo the screen's interface was barren except for the login fields. Female hands moved deftly over the keyboard typing characters into the computer. A tap of the 'Return' key and the screen changed to a list of menus.

After navigating a warren of menus the user arrived at the satellite identification system. Under the title SAT-IS, the user began entering the search criteria for Vulcan 4. A moment later they were rewarded with a list of options. They selected number three; Status and Telemetry.

The user's slender fingers drummed lightly on the desk as she scanned Vulcan 4's summary screen. Position, altitude, ground speed, tilt and more all reported in green assuring her that Vulcan 4 was alive and well.

Next, the user scanned the menu options, in the form of cryptic acronyms, which cluttered the bottom of the screen until she found the desired option.

SAT-GPOS headlined the next screen proving an automated guidance system. The woman replaced the current longitude and latitude with a new set of coordinates. Then changed the value of the current altitude to zero.

Pressing 'Return' prompted the user with a verbose warning and highlighting 'zero' in bold, red. The warning finished by offering the user with two options, "press ESC to cancel or RETURN to proceed".

"What do you think?" she said to herself. After a moment of feigned indecision she pressed the 'Return' key.

The command was accepted and added to the automated maintenance command queue system which managed the mundane operations of keeping satellites in their correct position, running utility tests and other redundant tasks deemed below the skill levels of the technicians.

Seconds later the encrypted navigation commands were transmitted to Vulcan 4. In response, Vulcan 4 fired its number two and six navigation thrusters for less than a second and began its inevitable, and terminal, return to terra firma.

Believing their job done, the user signed out, not knowing they had activated a small chunk of programming code. A local subroutine embedded into the exiting programs for Vulcan 4. This wasn't part of the original software, or an addition created by any of the programmers on staff with the NRO. The subroutine had been skillfully introduced through a back-door hack and had only one purpose. Send an alert if Vulcan 4 left its position.

Nathan's phone sharply droned on the nightstand like an angry wasp trapped in a box. The screen lit the darkened bedroom in blue/white light. With something between a sigh and a groan Nathan rolled over and groped for his phone.

"I'm getting it," said Nathan as his hand blindly slapped the nightstand, feeling for his phone and sending a half empty water bottle bouncing off the floor.

Cursing under his breath he grabbed the phone and brushing his light brown hair out of his face, he cracked one eye open against the glare of the phone's screen and read the message. What he read brought him fully awake and out of bed.

As he stepped into his office the motion sensor checked the time at 2:18 AM and slowly brought up the room lights enough for Nathan to see his way around. The room consisted of a lone chair and wide desk crowded with computers and monitors.

Pushing the chair out of the way, Nathan squinted his brown eyes against the bright computer screen and began typing commands. Within seconds Nathan was looking at the NRO navigation screen for Vulcan 4. Switching screens, he brought up the satellite's communication status. In red letters it said *OFFLINE*.

Pursing his lips he activated another monitor, pulling up Vulcan 4's fuel status then cross-referenced its current location.

His phone began buzzing and he spared it a resentful glance before returning his full attention to the computer screen. He requested a plot map of Vulcan 4's reentry and point of impact.

His phone went quite for only a second then rattled, again, on the desk with an incoming call. He ignored it. The phone buzzed twice more before Nathan's computer screen displayed a graphed map of Vulcan 4's flight path and estimated area of arrival. The phone went silent as he studied the map.

Having seen everything the map had to tell him Nathan pulled his chair over and sat down with a groan, rubbing his stubbled face. Taking a deep breath he stared at the phone, waiting for the phone to renew it's nagging. This time he answered the call.

"We lost the signal," snapped an angry voice.

"I know," said Nathan evenly. "Vul..."

"What's going on?"

Nathan ignored the interruption and drew another deep breath. "Vulcan 4 has been moved."

"4 what?" demanded the voice. "I'm talking about the satellite. We can't connect to it."

"Vulcan 4 *is* the satellite," said Nathan. "Someone…"

"I'm coming over."

Nathan sat forward. The situation just took an ominous turn. "I'll get dressed."

The line was quiet for a long pause. Nathan could feel the wheels turning in the head of the person on the other end of the call until they broke the silence. "Did you have anything to do with this?"

Nathan opened a new window on his monitor and began typing. "Does that even make sense?"

"No." The line went dead.

On the screen, Nathan scrolled over and clicked on a skull and crossbones icon. A female voice spoke from the recessed speakers in the ceiling, "Identification required."

"Beware the Jabberwocky," answered Nathan.

"Identification accepted," said the automated voice. "Jabberwocky activated. Your message has been sent successfully."

Even though he was expecting it, Nathan jumped when someone pounded on his door. Opening the door, he stood out of the way, understanding his visitor was coming in whether he liked it or not.

"What do you know?" the visitor demanded, walking past Nathan as if he wasn't there.

On the heels of the visitor entered another man who looked beyond Nathan. His stoney, blank face turned as he quickly scanned the room. The visitor stood in the middle of the room as his companion did a quick glance through each doorway. Satisfied, he stood with his back against a wall and settled his unflinching eyes on Nathan.

"Hi Walt," began Nathan.

"Walter," the visitor said. "What happened to our network?"

"Walter," said Nathan. "Vulcan 4, the satellite, has been moved."

Walter stared hard at Nathan while he rubbed his hands together as if grinding the life out of a bug. "Don't waste my time making me ask questions."

Walter glowered at Nathan, but the short man in his rumpled suit and disheveled combover did not intimidate Nathan. It was who Walter represented that made him dangerous and Nathan understood he could toy with Walter only so much, but this time he had to take Walter deadly serious.

The year before, Walter had approached Nathan for a job that needed a "quiet touch". He said he represented an investment company, whose name was unimportant. They needed someone skilled in bio-neural and quantum lattice crypto security.

Nathan was unsettled that someone not only knew who he was, but they'd known where to find him. After every job Nathan burned his identity, dumped his equipment and relocated. He simply disappeared into a black hole. How they knew who and where he was meant he was dealing with powerful people and that kind of power meant they could be dangerous.

But he was also intrigued. Crypto security meant working with seriously high-end systems available only to major corporations, governments and military. Nathan first suspected Walter was contracting out of a secret intel branch of the government. He took the job because the money was good, but his primary goal was to find out who they were and how they tracked him down. That was a hole in his personal security he was going to plug.

Achieving his goals proved to be harder than he anticipated. Who ever these people were, they were good at keeping secrets. The jobs they gave him were always strongly compartmentalized, seemingly random, and unconnected. But Nathan was persistent and focused.

Over time and careful not to leave any trace of his snooping, Nathan data mined anything related to the jobs they gave him. A location, business, a date and time of day, an employee, or a building, etc. He compiled everything associated with the subject of each job. He ran though millions of data points and thousands of computing hours, but found nothing. One thing he was convinced of was this wasn't a government intelligence agency. They were good, but not that good. This was something deeper. Darker.

The catalyst that led Nathan to the answers he was looking for began with an unremarkable, week old news story about the suicide of Mr. Billamy McGhee. It wasn't his name that caught Nathan's attention, but the date. He'd been given a job the same day of the suicide. Break into the computer system for a metals testing lab and change the results for item #WEP-03B88 from *fail* to *pass.*

Nathan zeroed in on Mr. McGhee, who it turned out was a stress analysis engineer and a contractor for the U.S. Military. Delving into McGhee's electronic life, Nathan ignored the ordinary looking for anything out of place and he found it.

Buried in an obscure cloud storage site, filed under a fake name, McGhee has stashed several recorded conversations.

Scanning through the recordings Nathan learned someone was making McGhee fake test results, approve faulty weapon parts and inflate project budgets.

It sounded like the typical sabotage corporations do to each other in order to steal contracts, etc., but as he listened to McGhee's last recording he realized he was in the middle of something deadly serious.

Billamy: What you're telling me to do doesn't make sense. How is putting defective, possibly hazardous, equipment in our military's hands for the good of our country?

*Unknown voice: The **government** is defective and hazardous. It's little pushes like the military losing confidence in the government that help add up and eventually weaken it enough for change.*

Billamy: Wait, weaken? You said The Ring was going to make the country better.

Unknown voice: After the Vix gutted the leadership in our government things have gone from bad to worse.

Billamy: Yeah, but undermining the government... we're throwing gas on the fire.

Unknown voice: Exactly. Look at fools running this country. Grade school teachers, insurance salesmen, community organizers. They're children playing at being leaders. They have no vision, or courage to make meaningful decisions. We have to burn it down before we can put the right people in power.

Billamy: Nobody said anything about burn...

Unknown voice: Okay, poor choice of words. More like re-direct.

Billamy: No. Don't bullshit me. This isn't about saving anything. You're talking about a coup.

Unknown voice: ...

Billamy: Oh my gosh, I'm right.

Unknown voice: Open your eyes, McGhee! The government is trying to tread water while holding on to an outdated anchor that only worked for the founding fathers. Voting the right people into power one at a time will take years, maybe generations. Do you honestly think the country has that long?

Billamy: I'm not doing this. No way.

Unknown voice: McGhee...

Billamy: I'm done. Out. Don't contact me again.

Unknown voice: I want you to think long and hard before you make the wrong decision.

Billamy: Is that... are you threatening me? I have insurance, you know. You even come near me and I'll make sure everyone knows about The Ring and what they're doing.

Unknown voice: (long pause) That's a mistake.

The recording ended at 1:37 AM and Billamy McGhee was dead three hours later.

A chill began to trickle through Nathan. The more he uncovered the deeper his dread deepened.

The Ring was a secret organization that was quietly, subtly manipulating companies, individuals, organizations, banks, stocks, industries and politicians. Recruiting influencers, people of power, decision makers. Spreading its tendrils until it was in the perfect position to take power over America and he had been unwittingly helping in laying that foundation.

Nathan was many things, but not a revolutionary. His first instinct was to disappear. He had a lot of experience with that. Burn his current identity, dump his equipment, scatter his electronic footprint, and fade away like smoke in the breeze. He'd be safe, but an uninvited voice in his head wouldn't stop asking, *for how long?* They'd found him once. They might do it again.

His absence wouldn't stop The Ring. Someday they'd be powerful enough to make their move and take over the country. His mental picture of an totalitarian America holding complete power over everyone chilled him. They wouldn't forget his desertion. He'd be on their wanted list.

His second choice wasn't less worrisome than the first, but the combination of risk and matching his wits against them was strongly appealing. He could continue to do jobs for The Ring, and at the same time use his hacking skills against them. It would demand patience and cunning to slip into their systems, discover the head of the snake and little by little undermine The Ring until it collapsed from within. But, it only took one misstep, any reason to mistrust, or doubt his loyalty and he'd be a dead man.

He accepted the challenge. *Lets see how smart you guys really are.* And so he stayed, spied and hunted for the head of the snake.

One of his first jobs for The Ring was to create a secure communications system. After extensive research, Nathan suggested hacking into a near-obsolete NSA communications satellite. You couldn't get more secure than the NSA. The Ring agreed and gave him the go-ahead. Vulcan 4 was the perfect fit and now, almost a year later, someone had kicked a wasp's nest by bringing down Vulcan 4, but that didn't compare to the full blown panic rippling through The Ring's leadership.

The previous week Nathan had been sneaking though one of the many systems The Ring used and discovered an email that set off near hysteria through the upper ranks of The Ring.

The person who sent the email said they'd just discovered a classified detail about Vulcan 4. It carried an onboard database of key codes which it assigned to every email, voice, or video transmission that passed through it. Digging into this unusual feature revealed something catastrophic. Vulcan 4 was sending a copy of every transmission to the NSA. In other words, the NSA was unknowingly archiving every transmission sent and received by The Ring.

The Ring's one saving grace was that the NSA was bloated with multiple huge data storage farms and had neither the people or processing power to review every transmission that went into their facilities.

As good as he was, even Nathan didn't know Vulcan 4 secret archiving system.

The person explained in their email added that they didn't have sufficient clearance to access and delete The Ring's transmissions. That sent up a big, red flag in Nathan's mind. Whoever wrote this email meant The Ring had someone inside the NSA. Not only that, but his new revelation about Vulcan 4's archiving system wasn't exclusive to The Ring because someone just knocked it out of orbit.

The Ring didn't know who sabotaged the satellite's orbit, but Nathan knew they'd start their witch hunt with him. He was the one who recommended Vulcan 4. He hacked it and he programed their communications gateway.

The Ring's first order of business would be damage control. Nathan knew he had a small window of safety while they were focused on that. The hunt for the saboteur would come later.

Knowing The Ring's heightened paranoia over being breached, Nathan believed they would err on the side of better safe than sorry. Reasonable doubt was a death sentence.

Even though Nathan wasn't involved, he knew he'd have to act fast if he needed to disappear, but staying in The Ring's good graces was critical to his plans of crippling them. *Making them trust me is going to take more than saying I'm innocent. I'll need to prove it otherwise I'll be facing the inevitable interrogation at the hands of a psychopath.*

Nathan considered his handler, Walter. He was incompetent, a bully and a narcissist; qualities Nathan could manipulate if everything went according to plan.

"Somebody accessed Vulcan 4 and changed its trajectory," said Nathan. "I don't know who, or why." Walter frowned, unhappy with the lack of information. "I ran a rough plot," continued Nathan, "and baring any changes it'll come down near the eastern border of Algeria."

"Algeria?" said Walter. "Who the hell's in Algeria? Why there?"

"Your people hired me to piggy-back your comms onto the satellite," said Nathan. "What you do with it, I don't want to know."

Walter waved his hand sharply at Nathan and started pacing. "Doesn't matter. Someone must have learned we're using it."

"If they wanted to shut down your network why not ditch the satellite in the sea?" asked Nathan as he casually watched Walter out of the corner of his eye. "Why dump it in the middle of a desert where anyone could pick it up?"

Walter stopped pacing as his face paled. "They're after the files," muttered Walter.

"After what?" said Nathan.

"Never mind. You need to save it" commanded Walter.

"Save it," repeated Nathan flatly.

"Yes!" said Walter. "The satellite, uh, Vulcan 4. Put it back where it was."

Nathan stopped the impulse to laugh at the ridiculousness of Walter's ignorance, keeping his expression a blank page. "That's impossible."

"Nothing's impossible. We pay you to do the impossible," said Walter, nearly pleading. Walter took a breath and tugged on his jacket, removing the rumples. His hand went to his head, about to smooth his combover, but he detoured it to the back of his neck, pretending to ease his building tension. He glanced around to see if anyone had noticed.

"So, you want me to report back that you won't fix it?" said Walter.

"Walt," began Nathan, but the balding man's flush of red told Nathan this wasn't the right time to play with the little man. "...ter, I'm being honest with you. It's not just me. Nobody could do it. This is our Humpty Dumpty."

"You think my boss wants to hear nursery rhymes at, uh..." Walter snapped his fingers several times until the bodyguard took the hint and looked at his watch.

"Two, forty," grunted the guard.

"Two forty." continued Walter. "There's got to be something you can do."

Nathan had been waiting for Walter to finally ask this. Now was his opportunity to demonstrate he was part of the team, and just maybe gain deeper access to The Ring.

"I don't have the computing power, but maybe if I had access to a serious mainframe I might be able to change where it lands, but," paused Nathan as Walter hung on his words, "I don't."

Walter's security man tensed as Nathan stepped towards the kitchen. "I'm getting coffee," said Nathan, unimpressed. "You want some Walter?"

"A mainframe," muttered Walter to himself. "The ranch's got big computers. Could be mainframes."

"Did you say something?" called Nathan from the kitchen.

"Yes," said Walter loudly then realized Nathan wasn't in the room. "You have coffee?"

"Yes," said Nathan.

Walter momentarily lost his scowl, but quickly remembered why he was there. "Mainframe," said Walter under his breath. "You," said Walter pointing to his guard, "I want a three man team, and uh, tell them to meet us at the ranch."

"What's the job, sir?" asked the guard.

"The job is, uh, to do what I tell them to do." Snapped Walter.

"No, sir," said the guard carefully. "I mean..."

"I know what you mean," said Walter just now understanding what the guard was asking. "Keep an eye on this glib prick," said Walter.

"Protect, or confine?"

"Both," said Walter impatiently. He quickly crossed to the kitchen door as Nathan was taking cups out of a cupboard.

"Put mine in a travel mug," ordered Walter. "Lots of cream."

Nathan paused with the coffee pot in his hand and looked over his shoulder, arching his eyebrow at Walter.

"Travel mug?"

"I'm taking you to a mainframe."

3

THE RANCH

The black sedan kicked up plumes of dust as it raced along the dirt road followed closely by a large SUV. Early morning light painted the barren, rolling landscape in hues of pink, purple and gold. There was nothing but desert as far as the eye could see.

Heat waves shimmered in the distance giving the illusion of motion to scrub and cactus. The cars crunched over the bleached remains of two bodies laying halfway in the road without notice, or slowing.

Several minutes later the road rose to a crest before dropping into a tiny canyon. Tucked against the shallow canyon walls was a long, squat ranch house. The windows were shuttered, but intact and a deep porch overhung the front of the ranch's dusty siding and brickwork keeping it in constant shade.

The cars swung into the empty yard and stopped. Before the dust could settle a woman and two men immediately got out of the SUV. Their dark suits and sun glasses sharply contrasted with the dull tan and faded reds of the desert surroundings.

Their shoes rapped sharply as they walked across weathered planks of the porch to the front door.

The woman flipped up a small cover on the wall next to the front door exposing a keypad. She punched in a series of numbers as Nathan, Walter and his guard got out of the sedan.

Nathan stretched his legs while taking in his surroundings. He had no idea where he was, but he was sure nobody would hear him yell for help. Walter's guard grumbled something and herded towards the ranch house.

Pressing the last button, the woman heard the subtle hum of a motor followed by a crisp *CLICK*. Opening the door, she and the two men walked inside, holding the door for Walter and his party.

Dingy light filtered through the cracks in the boarded up windows revealing a living room that smelled of old fabric and dust. They walked past the worn and dated furniture into a narrow hallway. Little light leaked into the hallway for Nathan to catch much detail except for a framed paint-by-numbers painting of a clown.

The hallway ended with another door where the woman revealed another keypad. Nathan heard the door unlock and was ushered into a dark room. The air was surprisingly fresh and cool. Blips of different colored lights winked at him from the walls in every direction. Someone pressed a switch and the room lights blazed to life making Nathan momentarily squint. His eyes quickly adjusted and saw several tall cabinets of computer equipment lining the walls. Across from where he came in was another door, but nobody was moving to open it. Against the left wall was a desk, several blank monitors, keyboards and a chair.

"You need a mainframe," said Walter, "you got a mainframe. Now, get to work."

Nathan crossed the room and sat in the chair taking a moment to get his bearings. He tapped one of the keyboards and the monitors came to life. "It's going to take a minute to tie into Vulcan 4's navigation system," explained Nathan.

"I don't need the, uh, play by play," said Walter. "Just let me know when you're..."

"I'm in," said Nathan with a satisfied smile. "This is an impressive system." A moment later each monitor was filled with Vulcan 4's status data. "I found it," he said as he brought up a graphic of thin, multicolored Ring's on a large monitor. Dotted among the Ring's were small diamond symbols with a six character label next to each one. "That's Vulcan 4," said Nathan pointing to an orange colored diamond. Vulcan 4 was moving, very slowly, along a line of dashes. "These dashes are Vulcan 4's current path," said Nathan. It's just passing into medium earth orbit."

"Do you have control of it?" asked Walter.

Nathan's fingers moved quickly over the keyboard as he leaned forward looking expectantly at one of the closer monitors. "Just a second," said Nathan.

Streams of meaningless characters began filling the monitor, but Walter understood that Nathan was somehow communicating with it.

The characters stopped and was replaced by an incomprehensible grid of acronyms and numbers. Nathan sat back in his chair with a sigh. "Yes, I've got control."

"Great," smiled Walter as he nodded to the blank expressions of the security guards. "Good. Okay, now fix it."

"You mean put it back in its original orbit?" said Nathan.

"Yes," confirmed Walter. "That's why you're here. That's why we pay you. You're the guy everyone says is a, uh, techno genie." Walter pointed at Vulcan 4's symbol on the screen. "This is where it is," he said then moved his finger to the ring, now above the orange diamond. "And this is where I want you to put it."

Walter's next words were interrupted by the buzz of his phone. He flashed his palm at Nathan as he answered the phone with his free hand. "Hello?"

Walter straightened up and glanced briefly at Nathan before turning his back on him. Walter tried to keep his conversation private, but the size of the room didn't allow it. "Yes, we're here," said Walter. "I told him to fix it, but uh, he says he can't."

"*Can't, or won't?*" demanded the caller.

Nathan stared at Walter's back making him hunch his shoulders as if to further mask his words. "He says someone hacked the satellite and took it off course. No, he doesn't know who."

Nathan didn't reflect the concern that was beginning to grow inside him with every glance Walter gave him. He only heard Walter's side of the conversation, but the mans posture said he was getting ready to throw Nathan under the bus.

"If that damn thing falls into the wrong hands all of us will be hanging from trees!" said the caller. *"What if Nathan learned about the satellite database? He's not one of us. I warned you not to hire him. He could be selling our info to anyone."*

"That information is compartmentalized," said Walter. "He wouldn't know that and if he does, then damn it, it wasn't me. Somebody over there screwed up big time." Walter began shaking his head in silent disagreement. "I can point fingers too."

"We're past that," said the caller. *"We have to clean house of every suspect. Kill him. Now. We'll talk about your decision to hire him later."*

Walter could barely suppress the whine in his voice. "I'm saying my guy's solid, okay? We can work on those answers after I fix this satellite thing. I gotta go."

"The moment he says it's fixed," said the caller, *"kill him."*

"Okay," said Walter and hung up. He folded his arms across his chest, staring expressionless at Nathan. The longer it went on the more awkward Nathan felt. He couldn't tell if Walter was trying to psych him out, or lost in his own thoughts.

"Did they decide what they want to do about Vulcan 4?" said Nathan, hoping he touched the right nerve.

"I'm the one with boots on the ground," snapped Walter. "I make the decisions and I want you to put it back."

"I can't," said Nathan with a sigh.

"Can't, or won't?" growled Walter.

"Vulcan 4 is descending through hundreds of miles of junk filled space. Pieces of other satellites, booster rockets, fragments the size of softballs to objects the size of a car and they're circling the planet up to seventeen thousand miles an hour," said Nathan moving his hands around an invisible globe. "Calculating a safe corridor through that flying demolition derby takes way more computer power than we have here, and even if we could it could be months before those bits of junk aline for a clear path." Nathan pointed to Vulcan 4's symbol on the monitor. "And while all of that is happening Vulcan 4 will drop lower and lower. The lower it gets, the stronger Earth's gravity pulls and that means you'll need a lot of thrust to break free. You're going to need a *lot* of fuel, and that's the one thing Vulcan 4 has little of."

Walter glared at the computer monitor while chewing the inside of his lip. Nathan had just dumped a heaping pile of 'no win' in Walter's lap.

"Then making us bring you out here was a waste of time," said Walter. He put his hands on his hips, under his jacket and turned away from Nathan to conceal his right hand edging towards his holstered gun. "I thought you were part of the team, but you've just been stalling us this whole time."

"I knew we couldn't save Vulcan 4," said Nathan calmly even as Walter glanced meaningfully at his security team. They took notice and straightened in anticipation of Walter's next orders.

"But I had you bring me here to confirm that we can protect The Ring from whoever did this," said Nathan, "and we can." Typing a few commands into the computer brought up Vulcan 4's projected target area.

Walter stroked his combover with his empty hand as he turned back to Nathan with renewed interest.

"Whoever brought Vulcan 4 out of orbit specifically chose this crash site," said Nathan. "I don't know why," lied Nathan, "and I don't want to know, but someone thinks there's something on that satellite worth having."

Walter looked dubious, but cautiously optimistic. "Let's say, for the moment, that's what it looks like to me, too," said Walter. "What can we do about it?"

"Vulcan 4 doesn't have enough fuel to return to its original orbit, but its got enough to change where it comes down," smiled Nathan.

Walter stared blankly at Nathan. "That's it? That's your big save?"

"I change its course and lock out its systems so nobody can take control of it," explained Nathan. "We'll be the only ones who can track it."

"Great," quipped Walter. "We can all sit around and watch our satellite crash."

"We'll also be the only ones who know where it is," added Nathan.

Walter's eyebrows rose as finally put the pieces together. "We'll be the only ones who know where to pick it up," grinned Walter as he excitedly paced back and forth. The security team's posture subtly relaxed and they stopped staring at Nathan.

"Its orbital path limits our options of touch-down," said Nathan as he began quickly typing a string of commands into the computer. Then turned back to Walter. "We can put it down in the ocean, or somewhere in the north of South America."

"Yeah, ditch it in the ocean," said Walter, but then shook his head, changing his mind. "No! Not the ocean. South America. Yeah, there."

Nathan turned back to the keyboard and began typing. "I'm giving Vulcan 4 a shallow trajectory which will delay its reentry by several days," said Nathan. "That should make it easier to predict its target area." A nearby monitor scrolled a list longitude and latitudes. "All right," said Nathan getting out of his chair and stretching his back.

Walter looked at the list of numbers over Nathan's shoulder, pretending to understand them. "So that's it?" said Walter veiling his hand reaching for his gun. "We just wait until numbers stop and they'll tell us where to find the satellite?" Walter's hand closed around the grip of his gun. His breathing became shallow as thumbed the safety off and slid the pistol out of the holster.

Nathan looked at his watch and yawned, unaware of Walter's movement. "Yeah," said Nathan.

Walter held the barrel of his gun inches from the back of Nathan's skull. He turned away from the inevitable spray of gore as he put is finger on the trigger.

"It won't be an exact location," said Nathan. "But we can narrow it down to a radius of a few hundred miles," added Nathan.

Walter subconsciously clenched his jaw as put his gun hand behind his back. "It could take years to crawl through four hundred square miles of jungle," frowned Walter. "You have to narrow down its location."

"As Vulcan 4 comes down, it's being subjected to all kinds of variable forces," said Nathan. "Gravity presses down on the earth's atmosphere, making it denser and creating friction. Every inch that force bounces Vulcan 4 can throw it off miles. Now add cross turbulence caused by gradient pressure forces which will push it all over the place. Then there's the drag created by the sat..."

"For a computer guy," said Walter, "you know an awful lot about satellites and space stuff."

"Calm down Walter," said Nathan. "I know a lot about lots of things. That's why people like you hire people like me."

Walter squeezed the gun behind his back until his knuckles turned white. He was nervous about facing his boss, who was dressing up Walter as the scapegoat for this serious breach of security, and frustrated with Nathan's smug calmness, as if it was just another day.

Last chance, thought Walter. *Say something useful, or I'll show you why they hire people like me.* "Four hundred miles," stated Walter. "That's the best you can do. Even with this monster computer and all your brains. A little gravity and winds got you beat."

Nathan was tired and losing patience with Walter's complaining. He just wanted to go home and sleep. All he had to do was tell Walter there was nothing else he could do. *Walter'd be mad, but the troll's always mad about something. He'll have to take me back home.*

"Yes, well," started Nathan but paused before finishing.

Walter's mind flashed forward the next few seconds of a flash of light, ringing ears and blood.

Almost unwanted, a possible solution began forming in Nathan's mind. He sighed dejectedly as realized he had an answer which meant he wouldn't be seeing his bed anytime soon. "I can narrow it down," said Nathan and turned back to the computer monitor. Walter straightened up and eased the gun back into his holster, forcing his stiff fingers to let go.

Nathan tapped the desk with a pencil as he worked out the details of his solution. "I'll adjust Vulcan 4 into a very shallow trajectory. It will take several passes around the earth using the density of the atmosphere to decelerate. The computer can refine its estimate with each pass which means a smaller crash radius."

"If we're tracking it right now," said Walter, "why don't we track it *after* it comes down?"

"We're tracking Vulcan 4's telemetry," said Nathan. "The heat of reentry will fry that system long before it comes down."

The skin over Walter's face drew taut with frustration at Nathan's answer. Walter could imagine his future, or lack of one, being decided by his superiors at this very moment. He'd have to give his boss a substantial better solution than four hundred square miles. "How long will it take?"

"Two days," said Nathan. "Maybe three."

Finally Walter had something solid to stand on and eagerly took control.

"You're gonna stay here until you have that landing area narrowed down a hell of a lot more than four hundred," said Walter brusquely. "You understand?"

"Here?" said Nathan. "This place's a dive. Why don't I come back in a couple of days and check the computer?"

"I want your undivided attention on this," said Walter. "You already have that."

"And I'm making sure it stays that way," said Walter. "And these guys are going to keep you company."

Nathan ignored the impulse to roll his eyes. He didn't want Walter knowing this is exactly what he wanted him to do. With the inspiration of slowing down Vulcan 4 to get a tighter crash location came the idea of how to turn the downing of the satellite to his benefit.

"What happens after I confirm the landing area?" asked Nathan.

"Then we send our people to get it," said Walter suspiciously. "Why're you so curious about what we do with the satellite?"

"I meant when I'm done here," said Nathan. "Can I go home then?"

"Oh, uh, yeah, I know what you meant," said Walter. "I take you back home," he lied. Walter tried to stare meaningfully at Nathan, but gave up. He turned to his security team as he pointed at Walter. "He stays here until I tell you otherwise."

Walter stopped in front of the closed door, his fingers tapping in annoyance on the side of his leg. "Hey," he said to his bodyguard, nodding his head at the door. The bodyguard quickly opened the door, letting Walter walk out, then followed.

4

CARDS ON THE TABLE

The room erupted in cheers and groans as the Saints intercepted a hail-mary pass from the Rams rookie quarterback. The sports announcer's words blurred into a single sound as he reported all the action.

Tate gently pushed the beer bottles and half empty snack bowls out of the way to make room and put his feet up on the stained and battered coffee table.

An easy smile creased his face as the sounds of people having a good time brought up memories of life before the Vix; parties with friends, easy camaraderie, and... just living. Small, almost trivial moments with his wife and daughter were now priceless. Swinging his daughter round and round until her small body lifted into the air. Her wild giggles as she held his hands. "Don't let go," she laughed. "I promise," he chuckled.

Frigid darkness poured into his mind, smothering all light. In one moment his life ended when his daughter was butchered right outside his front door. *Outside MY house! How did a Vix get there? I should have been home. Should have been; a real father would have.* Tate's guilt was blind to the realities of his life then. A highly trained and seasoned operator with Delta Force, Tate could be sent on a mission at any time and it was while he was away when his young daughter was killed by a Vix.

He couldn't forgive himself and hated himself even more when others told him he wasn't responsible. Plagued with grief, he convinced himself that his wife and everyone he knew secretly condemned him and would be glad to never see him again. The burdens he heaped on himself ultimately broke him. In the dark of night he abandoned his life, wife, comrades and friends, along with his self respect.

Two years of self loathing had settled into a dull apathy. Out of money, homeless and hungry, he signed up for the AVEF. It didn't matter that he was fat, out of shape and didn't give a damn about anything. Tate was just another warm body that could carry a gun.

How long ago that seemed. Almost like it was another person. Never in a million years would he have thought he'd care about anyone, or anything. It just proved how wrong he was... again. Now he was leading a team of rookie operators waging a covert war to destroy the very organization that created his team. The Ring.

Colonel Earl Hewett was recruited into The Ring by a friend who mysteriously died the day after calling Hewett; frightened of something he'd just learned about The Ring. This sparked off a chain of events leading Hewett to recruit Tate and form an alliance to bring down The Ring from the inside.

In spite of swearing to himself that he'd never be responsible for someone else's life again, here he was. Looking around the room at the happy faces he caught himself smiling. Accusations sprang into his mind, wiping the smile off his face. *Do you think they'd be smiling if they knew who you really were? What you've done?*

Monkhouse plopped down on the couch next to Tate, breaking his thoughts and bouncing bits of corn chips and popcorn off the cushion.

"You know, it's not about the fame and medals," said Monkhouse, with a sloppy grin, pointing to the handmade paper medals everyone had taped to his shirt. He was the one who came up with the idea of hacking the cable feed and even designed the device to do it with. In gratitude, the team had cut out paper medals and thrown an awards ceremony for him.

Monkhouse waved his beer bottle, pointing to the others in the room. "Any of these guys could be a hero, am I right, Top? I mean, yeah, okay, nobody else would'a figured out how to tap into that cable feed, or got us free TV, but..." Monkhouse noticed the debris of snacks he'd kicked up onto Tate's leg and picked up a, mostly, whole chip. "You gonna eat this?"

Tate grinned in spite of himself and shook his head. "It's all yours, cowboy."

Monkhouse wobbled his head in thanks and tried to synchronize his hand and mouth to steer the chip into his mouth, but gave up after breaking it on his chin. Looking back at Tate, his eyes lit up remembering what he was going to say. "All of us are heroes in our own way," Monkhouse said pointing his beer bottle at himself, spilling beer on his chest. "And nobody's perfect. We all done bad things; on purpose and mistake."

Tate frowned at Monkhouse's unexpected insight. That had hit close to home. "Can we ever make up for our sins?" asked Tate in a moment of unguarded thought. Realizing his blunder he glanced around fearing everyone had heard him. His darkest sins exposed, they'd exile him from their lives. But nobody heard, and the good cheer still filled the room. That is, except for Monkhouse who didn't see the deeper meaning to Tate's question.

"Make up for it?" Monkhouse repeated thoughtfully. "Maybe we can, you know, balance it out with good deeds. Sort of pay off the bad karma." Monkhouse poked Tate's shoulder good naturedly with his new revelation. "Life's full of second chances. Just between us, I've done..." Monkhouse seemed to catch himself and glance guilty around the room. "...stuff. But Karma knows me, you, all these guys... we don't walk on water. Just broken a little. That's what we are. We're impervious heroes."

"You mean imperfect?" prompted Tate.

"That's what I said," frowned Monkhouse. "Imperfect heroes."

Tate enjoyed a deep breath of night air while walking to his quarters. The stillness of the night was a sharp contrast to the party he'd just left and left his mind dwelling on Monkhouse's words. Maybe there was some truth to what he'd said.

"Everything okay, Sergeant Major?"

It took a second for Tate to get his bearings. A young MP was standing in front of him with his hand resting on his radio as a precaution.

Tate realized he must have been standing there for a while lost in thought until the MP noticed him. "I got a little turned around," said Tate. "I just got new quarters and was heading to my old one before I caught myself."

The MP's stiff posture loosened a little now that he knew he wouldn't have to deal with a drunk, and possibly uncooperative Sergeant Major. "The new quarters are over there," he said pointing with his flashlight. "Would you like directions?"

Tate chuckled. "I'm not that lost."

"Have a good night, Top," said the MP.

"Same," said Tate heading to his quarters.

The army base, Fort Hickock, was in the process of expanding its permanent housing starting with the commissioned officers and senior NCOs. Tate had won a lottery, being picked for one of the first available, new, NCO quarters.

Located at the southern most end of Panama, the Fort Hickock was situated to act as a barricade stopping the flow of Vix wandering out of South America which had been catastrophically overrun by Vix in the early days of the outbreak.

The southern fortifications, facing the brunt of Vix swarms, bristled with machine guns, grenade launchers and 20mm cannons. In earlier days every gun was manned twenty four hours a day to defend against the random swarms that would shamble out of the jungle. Underestimating the horror these frail looking and lethargic creatures could instantly unload on you was a mistake you'd be lucky to live through.

Early into the outbreak Tate was stranded on the roof of a

sporting goods store waiting for a wandering herd of Vix to eventually pass through what was left of a small town in New Mexico.

The stench of spoiled food from the abandoned Indian take-out across the street had attracted a large pack of feral dogs. Seeing the Vix, the dogs came out to defend their territory. Hackles raised, the dogs began growling and snarling. It was like flipping a switch. Triggered by the sounds, the meandering, nearly inert Vix transformed into an seething mass of lightening savagery. Driven by hunger, the dogs attacked. In seconds the Vix ripped through the pack like a flash flood. One of the dogs panicked and bolted, at full run, down the street, yelping in terror. Tate's jaw dropped as two Vix raced after the animal, easily catching up and pounced on it.

Another dog scrambled through a small hole in the side of a store. Feeling safer the dog snarled and snapped at the hands reaching for it. This whipped the Vix into a frenzy and they began attacking the adobe wall of the store, gashing chunks out of the soft brick until they'd wrecked their arms to jagged stumps of bone and still they came. In less than a minute they tore through the wall and flooded into the store. The spectacle left Tate melancholy, realizing although he'd been captivated by the drama, he'd been rooting for the dog. He got up to head back to his makeshift tent when he caught sight of the dogs head pop out between the bars of a window. It shimmied and squirmed until it got free of the bars and took off. Tate's spirit rose as he silently cheered the dog on. *A win for the good guys.*

Now, two years after the outbreak science still understood little about the Vix. The fear of infection was so great that scientific research on Vix was outlawed within populated areas. Not even tissue samples were allowed. The researchers who dared to venture outside of the protective walls of civilization were few and any advancement in studying Vix biology was hampered by an absence of supporting resources. The general consensus was that the Vix would eventually rot away in a few years, give or take and nobody, who had money, wanted to put money into a self-correcting problem.

Tate's experience contradicted that theory. The Vix didn't decay normally. They were fast and strong. His hand subconsciously rested on his Colt 1911 as his memories of the undead filled his head.

It wasn't until he closed the door behind him and switched on the lights to his quarters that he appreciated how much he'd spooked himself during his walk.

He'd been out of communications with Hewett since before their cable hacking mission and decided he'd see if there was any notices on his satellite phone before heading to bed.

The sat-phone was his direct comms to Colonel Hewett. Their lives depended on The Ring never knowing they were, of a sorts, double agents. Their sat-phones used strong encryption guaranteeing their conversations were secure.

Hewett had been keeping a low profile since the last mission. With inside information Hewett had stolen from one of the members, Tate and the Grave Diggers sabotaged a major deal, costing The Ring a few million dollars and the suicide of a suspected member. Both Tate and Hewett had agreed to wait for the ripples of that mission to die out before taking on another. Every organization knew plans sometimes failed, even disastrously on occasion. But too many disasters would attract the wrong kind of attention from The Ring; something Tate and Hewett wanted to avoid.

Tate punched in the combination to a small safe and took out the sat-phone and battery. Snapping in the battery he paused, watching for the power to come on. He put it down to take off his boots while waiting for the sat phone to link to a satellite. Halfway though untying his second boot the sat phone chimed. It always did that when it powered on and he ignored it, continuing to undo his boot. The sat-phone chimed again. Then again, and again. *It didn't always do that.*

Tate forgot about his boot and grabbed the sat-phone. The display showed multiple calls and voice mail from the same number, but it wasn't Hewett's.

Questions swirled around his head. *Am I compromised? Should I warn the team? Has Hewett gotten the same call?*

Hoping the voicemail message would answer his questions Tate selected the message on the menu and pressed *play*.

"Hello Sergeant Major," began the recording. Tate frowned as he tried to put a face to this familiar voice. "This is Nathan. Yes, the same Nathan you rescued from San Roman."

Tate's eyebrows rose in surprise.

"I need your help. I'm being held prisoner by two or more guards. Go to locker 1171 in the train station in Temple, Texas for further instructions. The combination is five, eighteen, ten. Hurry, Sergeant Major. My time is limited, and yes, the irony is not lost on me. In case you're deciding if I'm worth the trouble you should know I have critical information which could potentially destroy The Ring. And whatever you do, do not force open the locker."

Wesson propped her elbow on the table and rested her chin in her palm while Kaiden did nothing to hide a yawn.

Tate turned the sat-phone off having just played Nathan's message for them. He waited a few moments to let them form an opinion.

"This is why you got me out of bed?" said Kaiden squinting at Tate with her almond shaped eyes.

"At least you were *in* bed," said Wesson.

"You'll get a chance to sleep it off," said Kaiden.

Wesson lifted her head, throwing bleary daggers at Kaiden.

"Lets get back on point," injected Tate before Wesson could reply. "What do you think? Rescue him, or not?"

"Could be a trap," said Kaiden. "We know he works both sides."

"But we saved his life once before," said Tate. "He said he'd work with us."

"Is that enough for you to trust him?"

"No," grunted Tate, "but it's enough if he has intel that can wreck The Ring... I think that's worth the risk. Wesson?"

"I don't even know who this is," said Wesson. "Or, San Roman, or what op you ran without me. If you want to exclude me, it's not my place to complain, but I feel like a third wheel in this team." Wesson lingered on Kaiden making her meaning clear to Tate.

He was caught off guard by Wesson's break from her usual adherence to military formality. He understood the beers were doing the talking, but there was some truth in her words.

"Sergeant, you're my second in command for a reason," said Tate. "I kept you and the rest of the team out of the loop for your own safety, but that was then. Now the team knows what we're up against and accepts the risks. You're *in* the loop now, and I'm asking your opinion whether we go, or not."

Wesson straightened up, blinking her eyes clear. "All right," she said looking at the table thoughtfully. "We don't know where we're going."

"Right," said Tate.

"We don't know how many hostiles there are, or how their armed."

Tate simply nodded.

"And it's a 50/50 chance this is a set up to hand us over to The Ring."

"Sounds like half the missions I've been on," said Kaiden as she sat back in her chair and stretched.

"The reward of getting that info sounds too good to be real," said Wesson.

Tate was about to say something when Wesson finished her thought. "But that doesn't mean it's not." Glancing from the corner of her eye she saw Kaiden nodding in agreement. "We've been hurting The Ring, but not to the bone. This could be what we need to inflict real damage. I say we go," said Wesson, "but, be ready for an ambush." She looked at Tate wondering how he was judging her decision.

"Assemble the team," said Tate. "Brief them and have them get ready to deploy."

"Hey," said Kaiden. "You didn't ask what I thought."

"Kill bad guys? Steal top secret intel?" said Tate. "This missions got you written all over it."

A wicked grin spread from Kaiden's mouth to her eyes. "Yeah, it does," she said. "But how do we get the green light for transportation to pull an unsanctioned operation in Texas?"

Tate's shoulders dropped with a heavy sigh. Kaiden came fully awake instinctively reading Tate. "You're going to tell Hewett about this? About your connection to Nathan?"

"There's no way around it," said Tate. "This can't happen without his authorization."

"Once he's put together that you've been running off the book ops, you're exposing yourself to a huge risk," said Kaiden. "You've never been convinced of his loyalties. If he is genuine, everyone's happy. But... if he's loyal to The Ring the instant he knows you're after this intel it puts a bullseye on all of us."

"I have a contingency for that," said Tate grimly. "You don't have to be a part of this."

"Aw, aren't you sweet," laughed Kaiden, brushing her long black hair out of her face. "Try and keep me out of it."

Wesson read the cool determination in Kaiden's eyes with an subtle nod of approval.

"That's it, then," said Tate, standing up. "You two make ready. I'll call Hewett."

Hewett didn't hide his skepticism and it came through the sat-phone loud and clear. "A training mission. In Texas."

"Yes, sir," said Tate. "It's a great opportunity to improve the team's skill, get them out of their element, and test their abilities."

"Huh, I see," said Hewett, flatly.

Tate waited and listened as the colonel drew out the long silence until he broke it with a gravely sigh. "I'll tell you what I think," said Hewett, "I think you've been pissing in my ear for the last fifteen minutes and telling me it's raining, Sergeant Major."

Tate clenched his jaw, angry with himself. The colonel had known Tate was lying from the beginning and he let Tate dig himself into a hole.

Tate felt a palpable sensation from the other end of the call that the colonel was seeing through everything he was thinking. Like a bomb, Tate had armed the colonel's suspicions and another lie would

would be the spark that convinced him Tate couldn't be trusted, or worse, was a dangerous threat.

None of this was going to plan. He'd always considered the Colonel to be a blunt instrument, direct and to the point. Tate berated himself for such an obvious screw up. Hewett hadn't made it to Colonel without becoming skillful in playing politics in the military. *And I should have known that.*

Not for the last time did Tate condem himself falling so far from the lean, cunning warrior he once was. Now he was left scrambling, caught in a lie. His only way out was to give up the one thing protecting Tate, and his team, from the possibility that the colonel was a double agent for The Ring. The truth.

Tate and Kaiden knew how to go off the radar, but they'd be hunted for the rest of their lives. He'd do what he could for the rest of the team, but Tate knew they'd be found and killed.

He had to put his cards on the table, but now he would finally know if Hewett could be trusted, or not.

"I know what you're thinking," said Hewett.

"Sir?"

"You're deciding how much you need to tell me without exposing what you're really up to. That if I'm secretly allied with The Ring and I've been playing you, you'll try to kill me before I kill you."

"That's a serious accusation, colonel," said Tate. "What makes you think that?"

"Because I'd be thinking the same thing," chuckled Hewett. "Open your ears. This cloak and dagger crap isn't my style. I'm being forthright, sergeant major, and I expect the same from you. Right here. Right now. Make up your mind. Either we get to the business of killing each other, or we pull our heads out of our collective asses and get back to taking down The Ring."

Before now, Tate hadn't considered that Hewett was just as prepared to kill him if he sensed a double-cross as he was. If anything, it was a convincing argument for Hewett's credibility.

"The ball's in your court," warned Hewett. "Are we working together, or not?"

Listening to his gut, Tate took a deep breath and plunged in.

"Colonel, I have to rescue an informant who's in possession of intel that could severely damage The Ring," said Tate.

The line was quiet for so long that Tate began to suspect Hewett and hung up. "You have an informant inside The Ring and didn't tell me?" said Hewett.

Hearing the Colonel phrase it that way magnified Tate's practice of mistrust he had for Hewett. He realized the hole he'd dug for himself and the damage this could do to his alliance with Hewett. Tate threw a hail-mary excuse hoping it would work. "Not in that way, Sir," said Tate. "I compartmentalized information to protect everyone involved in case one of us were compromised... just as I assume you're doing the same with me."

Tate squeezed the sat-phone subconsciously expecting the worse. He could hear Hewett tapping his desk with something hard as he mulled over Tate's explanation.

"I appreciate the value you put on secrecy," said Hewett, carefully choosing his words, "providing it's for the right reason."

Tate silently breathed a sigh of relief.

"I honestly believe you and I are on the same side, that we both want to take down The Ring, but," growled Hewett, "take caution you don't shake my trust in you."

"I understand, Sir," added Tate.

"I sure as hell hope so," said Hewett. "Permission granted. I'll arrange transport to Fort Hood in Texas and provide the necessary authorizations for your operational needs."

"Thank you, colonel," said Tate. Relief washed through him and suddenly felt the lack of sleep press down on him.

"Sergeant Major," said Hewett, "don't draw attention to yourself. I don't know if The Ring has people on that army base, but it would be a grave mistake to assume they don't."

"I understand, sir," said Tate. "I'll report back after the operation."

"Good luck, Tate," said Hewett and hung up.

5

HOW THE OTHER HALF LIVES

Tate's chin drooped to his chest in spite of the droning roar of the C-130's four turboprop engines leaking through his headset. Even the bite of the unforgiving webbing of the backrest of his seat couldn't overcome his fatigue.

The military cargo plane bumped through an air pocket, jolting his head back, waking him with a start. Tate screwed his red rimmed eyes at his watch trying to figure out how long he'd been awake. Forty something hours as best he could guess. He groaned as plane banked, funneling a shaft of harsh sunlight through the opposite window into his face, pushing his thudding headache up another notch.

Squinting, he turned away looking down the aft of the cargo bay at the loading ramp. Memories of jumping from those ramps flipped through his mind. Night and day jumps into hostile territory. He relived that instant of stepping off the ramp, a half second of quiet then the kick from the prop-wash. After that nothing but the sound of rushing wind as he went into free fall. He made a mental note of training this team in parachuting to the ever growing list of things they needed to learn.

Tate had worked them hard from a loose collection of volunteers into a, mostly, cohesive team. The U.S. Army treated the All Volunteer Expeditionary Force as a bastard child made apparent by the ridiculously meager training they got in boot camp and the second hand equipment they were supplied.

The AVEF existed for the sole purpose of finding and shooting Vix. No combat training needed. Even the French Foreign Legion had higher standards than the AVEF.

No identification was required to join and no background check was made. What ever name you signed up with, real or invented, was how you were registered. When, or if, you survived your tour of duty you were discharged with a new identity which made the AVEF the perfect refuge for the dregs of the human race.

There was little Tate knew about his team's past. Wesson, the team's second in command, was a closed book and so was Ota, the teams sniper. Rosse said he had been a prison guard; Fulton worked on a farm, and Monkhouse, the teams engineer, was a... engineer? Based on what Tate had seen him do he might have been a legitimate engineer, or for that matter, a safe cracker, or a handyman with a thing for blowing stuff up. He didn't fault them for their secrets. He had his own and kept them close to the vest.

Kaiden, on the other hand, had been part of his Delta team back in his old life. She knew his family, hobbies and, of course, his real name. If she held any judgements about Tate she kept them to herself. It was a talent Tate appreciated, but it also irritated him. Even though they were friends Kaiden was... elusive. Her private life wasn't just private. It was secret. And somewhere behind that shroud, Tate suspected she was living another life. Kaiden would disappear for days and return without mentioning it. The few times Tate had pressed her about it she would smile and ignore him. Some of the guys on his old Delta team had joked that she was a spook, working for the CIA, and although Tate didn't like to make assumptions he suspected that was closer to the truth.

A quick movement caught Tate's attention as Fulton fumbled with his MP5, and the compact submachine gun clattered on the floor's metal plating. Blushing, Fulton quickly picked it up, shrugging apologetically to Tate. *Add weapons handling to the training list.*

The team did show progress in some areas. They could shoot and move better than the average combat soldier, but they weren't supposed to be average. Unofficially, their role was special operations and in spite of the improvements he saw in each of them there was a lot of blood, sweat and pain they'd go through before they'd reach the elite level he expected of them.

The plane bucked, shaking Tate from his thoughts. He wondered how long he'd been staring at the cargo ramp. Everyone appeared lost in their own thoughts. The team had deployed in the middle of the night, only a few hours after their party and it was anyones guess how much sleep they'd gotten on the flight except for the teams medic, Sergeant Tyler Rosse. He was asleep before they were wheels-up. His squat, barrel chested frame sagged like a rag doll in his chair. Tate simultaneously envied and resented the man.

His thoughts were broken as the pilots voice scratch over the headset.

"Attention back there," said the pilot. We're making our final approach to the Hood."

Tate notices a drop in the roar of the engines as the plane took another bank then settled down.

"Strap in," said the pilot. "We'll be wheels-down in two shakes."

"Somebody wake up Rosse," said Tate resisting the temptation to do it himself.

"Come on, dude," said Fulton pushing his elbow in Rosse's arm. "Wake up."

Private Jeff Fulton was the youngest member of the Grave Diggers and the team's radio man. Rosse had taken Fulton under his wing after a traumatic run-in with a ruthless band of scavengers. Fulton had been his shadow ever since. Rosse reluctantly accepted his new sidekick with his typical abrasiveness.

"Yeah, I'm up. I'm up," groused Rosse with his eyes still closed. Blinking, he sat up and stretched with a drawn out groan. Suddenly his eyes went wide as he looked up at the fat ducting that snaked along the overhead of the cargo bay.

"What is that?" exclaimed Rosse pointing to a sheet of white vapor coming down from the overhead pipes. "Is it supposed to do that?"

Everyone looked until they saw what Rosse was pointing at then returned to their own tasks, unconcerned.

"Relax," said Tate. "It's just vapor coming off the cooling system. It won't kill you."

"There's lots of stories about the military doing chemical experiments," added Fulton. "Maybe..."

Rosse frowned at Fulton who withered under his stair.

"But that was a long time ago," offered Fulton. "You know, if you believe that kind of stuff."

"Ya see this?" groused Rosse. "This is why I hate flying."

"It's a wonder you slept at all," Tate jibbed.

The floor of the plane bucked as the landing gear touched down. Everyone held on as the pilot reversed the engines. Whatever Rosse was complaining about was drowned out as the four, forty three hundred horse powered, engines rose to a deafening roar as they pushed against forty tons of speeding aircraft, quickly bringing its inertia to its taxi speed.

After several minutes of taxing across the airfield the C-130 gently bumped to a stop. Metal seatbelts clicked open as everyone got out of their seats with a stretch and a groan. Bracing against the gentle sway of the rolling plane they picked up their gear.

The brakes grumbled, bringing the plane to a stop. A moment later light and Texas heat spilled into the cargo bay as the loading ramp lowered to the tarmac.

Outside, two bored soldiers sat on the back of a flat-bed truck, indifferently watching the team come down the ramp.

Stepping out of under the shade of the plane the sun beat down on Tate. He fished out his weather beaten boonie hat for relief.

"I thought it would be cooler than home," said Wesson.

"Nah," said Fulton. "Jungle heat's got nothing on Texas."

"But, it's a dry heat," grinned Monkhouse.

Tate slung his pack over his shoulder and walked over to the soldiers on the truck who sized him up as he approached.

Looking at the team, nobody could be blamed for thinking they'd been dumpster diving at an army surplus store. Their worn and faded army combat uniforms were a collection of mismatched camo patterns. Their gear was functional but dated and their weapons, in some cases, were older than they were.

Nobody in the team, including Tate, wore their rank. On their ACU jacket was their name tape in faded black letters. The one thing that they all had in common was the unit patch each wore on their shoulder. A green shield with a red border. In the middle of the shield was a snarling skull with a black dagger plunged through it. Across the top of the shield was their unit motto, *Relentless Remorseless*. Anyone curious enough to look up the unit patch wouldn't find it, or for that matter, any unit named Grave Diggers. If anyone asked they were told the team was part of the AVEF. After that most people lost interest. The AVEF was considered the ugly, step-bastard of the US Army by many in the military. It was a bias that Tate tried to ignore, but admitted he probably would have shared that opinion when he was part of the elite Delta Force.

"Corporal Duggan," stated Tate, seeing the soldiers name and two chevrons on his uniform. "I'm picking up a vehicle," said Tate, showing him the manifest. "Can you tell me where the motor-pool is?"

"It's about four miles up that road," said Duggan, pointing with his thumb.

Monkhouse followed the soldiers direction with his eyes seeing only blurry, distant buildings through the shimmering heat. "Four *miles*?" repeated Monkhouse.

"What'sa matter? Can't take a little sun?" mocked Rosse, whose face was already running with sweat.

"Says the guy who looks like a snowman in hell," said Monkhouse.

"Can you give us a ride?" said Tate.

Duggan eyed Tate's ACUs for any sign of rank before answering. "I dunno," he said. "Can we?"

Tate smiled ironically. *The army's the same everywhere you go*, he thought. "How about we help you load up that cargo?" said Tate, nodding to the pallet of supplies in the cargo bay of the plane.

"Looks like you got yourself a ride," grinned Duggan.

Riding down Hell on Wheels avenue the team couldn't help be impressed by the size of the U.S. Army base, Fort Hood. To the north were vast parking lots holding row after row of military vehicles. To the south were building after building surrounded by parking lots. The Hood was a small city.

Tate rode in the truck's cab with Duggan while the other soldier, Private Eden sat in the back with the rest of the team. "I guess you don't see something like this where you're from," said Eden.

"How big is this base?" asked Fulton.

"The main base's about six miles," said Eden. "But there's miles of training grounds past that."

"No way," said Fulton. "And it's all walled off?"

"Nah," chuckled Eden. "Just the main base and most of the city. I wasn't here when the Vix hit, but the story is the base buttoned up like a bank vault. Once that was secure they mobilized everyone to save the city before the Vix wiped the place out."

"That musta been a helluva fight," said Rosse. "How'd it go?"

Everyone, except Eden, jumped as two helicopters thundered low overhead. Clusters of weapons hung off the sides giving them an insect quality.

Eden laughed as he pointed at the choppers, which had already shrunk to black dots in the distance. "About how'd you expect. The hard work was walling off the city. I got transferred here for that." Eden frowned as he looked off in the distance for a moment, but then brightened up. "Hey, we're going by the Post Exchange to drop off some of this stuff," he nodded to the pallet. "You guys want to check it out? Maybe get some new ACUs? No offense."

Everyone, but Kaiden, glanced at their weather faded army combat uniforms. Surplus uniforms were available at their own base, but often the camo was mismatched and the right size was hard to come by. Unlike the rest of the team, Kaiden's gear, from her boots to her weapon, were modern. It rankled Wesson that, although Kaiden was part of the team, she came and went as she pleased without a word from Tate. Wesson recognized Tate and Kaiden had history before the AVEF, but it was a surprise when Tate returned from an unexplained trip with Kaiden in tow. Although she dressed in camos, nobody knew and Tate didn't say if Kaiden was military. She didn't wear a rank, never formally gave orders, or saluted. Wesson didn't like unknowns and Kaiden represented a big one.

"We're on a time limit," said Wesson doing a better job at hiding her disappointment than the others. "We have to get our vehicle and head out."

"You got time," said Eden. "I know the guy running the motor pool and he's not there for another hour."

Wesson talked it over with Tate through the sliding rear window of the truck's cab. Tate looked at his watch with annoyance creasing his face, but realized it was out of his hands. With a nod and lopsided smile he gave Wesson a thumbs up.

The team couldn't help but gawk at as Corporal Duggan led them through the automatic, glass doors of the PX. The splendor of this indoor mall made their home PX look like a shack by comparison. This was nothing less than a sprawling, air conditioned, shoppers paradise.

"There's a food court down that way," said Duggan, pointing to one of the store lined corridors. "Personal gear..." Tate caught Duggan's quick glance at their appearance, but didn't take offense. "Uniforms, BDU's, packs, that kind of stuff are that way. You can check out the directory for anything else."

"Well, crap." said Rosse taking in the white polished flooring, modern decor and groomed people. "Don't I feel like a fart in church."

Eyeing his team, Tate saw how self conscience they felt, except for

Kaiden, which didn't surprise Tate at all. "We meet back here in 45 minutes," he said. "If you're late you're walking home."

The truck's breaks squealed to a stop outside the motor pool's office and the team climbed off the flatbed. Tate came around to the driver's door and shook Duggan's hand. "Thanks for everything," said Tate, handing Duggan a fold of bills.

"Yeah, no problem," said Duggan with a smile. "Look me up next time you're on base if you need anything."

"Will do," said Tate with a wave. He joined his team under the shade of broad awning covering a couple mechanics working on an armored personal carrier.

Tate spotted a sullen looking corporal halfheartedly pushing a broom.

"Excuse me, corporal," said Tate, showing him the vehicle requisition. "Who do I see about getting this?"

"Fourteen weeks of combat training," groused the corporal, "and they make me a janitor."

"Welcome to the army," chuckled Tate sympathetically.

"Yeah, no kidding," said the corporal. He eyed the form Tate showed him and nodded his head towards a set of nearby doors.

"The Chief's inside," said the corporal, nearly spitting the words.

"Thanks," said Tate and headed inside.

Tate smiled ironically as he glanced around the motor pool office. The inside of every army building he'd ever been in looked like it had been decorated by an interior designer suffering from near clinical apathy. It brought the word 'drab' to a new, all time, low.

Tate walked up to the counter where stacked trays, containing colored forms, sat in rows on his left and right. Taped to the wall was a sheet listing the form numbers for each tray. A black, plastic binder sat prominently on the counter with "Read first, then ask" written on the front. Next to that was another handwritten, paper sign taped to the counter, "Ring for service" with an arrow pointing to an empty space. Everything about the place said *not welcomed*. Behind the counter Tate saw a wide figure in the back office. He knew the person had seen Tate, but made no move to get up or acknowledge him.

"I'm here to pick up a vehicle," called out Tate.

With an audible sigh the Chief looked up from his desk and fixed Tate with a disapproving expression of everything Tate had ever done and would ever do in his life including his decision to be in the chief's motor-pool.

Tate saluted respectfully as the chief pushed himself away from his desk with a grunt and returned the salute as an afterthought. He picked up the requisition and examined it.

"Cab mounted AI camera," said the chief as he read down the load out list. "Night vision, parabolic mic... that's a lot of gear to roll around in."

Although he'd received a copy of requisition the day before, the chief sounded like it was the first time he'd seen it. Tate sensed the chief was fishing for why he needed all of that equipment and was happy to leave him hanging.

"Is it ready?" asked Tate.

"Are you qualified in a PLAV?" asked the chief.

It was a fair enough question. The Platoon Light Assault Vehicle was more than an up-armored SUV and the time to learn how to use it wasn't in the middle of combat. But the chief's question was also a reminder that the person who ran the motor pool held the keys to the kingdom. Sure, the Army paid for all of these vehicles, but once they put them in the hands of the chief they belonged to him, and everyone from the greenest of privates to top ranking generals knew it.

"Yes, sir," said Tate. "Where do I sign?"

The chief slid a form onto a clipboard and let the clip close with a loud snap.

"It's fueled, and fully functional," said the chief pointing to the signature line on the form. "That's how you bring it back."

"Wouldn't have it any other way," smiled Tate.

The chief came around the counter and out the door with Tate behind. The bright Texas sun making them blink and renewing his headache from a dull throb to a banging drum. He put on his sunglasses instantly easing the stabbing pain in his eyes. He'd been awake for a day and a half and it was wearing him down. Tate cursed himself for wandering around the post exchange instead of sleeping.

"Corporal," called the chief. "Bring out the PLAV in bay three."

The team watched the disgruntled corporal prop his broom against the wall and disappear inside a garage bay. A moment later they heard a low growl and the solid bulk of the Platoon Light Assault Vehicle rumbled out like huge beast emerging from its lair. The chunky, armored body of the PLAV rode on four giant dragon-scale, run-flat tires. The cab sat four and a half feet off the ground with a thick, armored windshield that scowled over the stout, brooding hood and reinforced grill.

Monkhouse exclaimed something and pulled himself onto the running board of the PLAV before it'd stopped. "Have you ever seen anything more beautiful?" said Monkhouse. "I read about these."

"Aw crap," said Rosse. "Here we go."

"Eight liter, turbodiesel engine," continued Monkhouse, lovingly patting the armored side. Five hundred horse power, zero to sixty in four point eight seconds."

The chief looked at Tate with misgivings.

"He doesn't get out much," sighed Tate.

"30 millimeter cannon with..." Monkhouse stopped, scanning the roof of the cab. "No cannon? Hey Top, we don't have a canon."

"Load up, everyone," said Tate. "Monkhouse, you're up front with me."

One by one the team scrambled up the side of the PLAV and through the thick doors, closing them with a solid *thunk*.

Tate sat behind the wheel scanning the array of screens and buttons crowding the dashboard. Next to him Monkhouse's eyes shined excitedly as he took in the control console.

Hey, uh, Monkhouse..." said Tate under his breath. "Do you know which one's the ignition?"

"No," said Monkhouse grinning. "But isn't this great?"

Suddenly Kaiden leaned in between them, from the troop compartment, and pressed a button near Tate's hand. The PLAV's engine growled to life; sensors, displays and switches all lit up.

"Anything else?" asked Kaiden with mock innocence.

Tate tried to glare at her, but it felt anemic. The military had advanced its technology in the time since he'd abandoned his old life and even though it wasn't her fault he felt stupid sitting there, and he wished she wouldn't keep reminding him.

"Change of plans," grumbled Tate. "Monkhouse, you're in the back.

"Is that an invitation?" smiled Kaiden.

"Don't rub it in," said Tate and turned his attention back to the dashboard and waited as Kaiden climbed into the passenger seat.

6

OUTSIDE THE WALL

Once outside the protection of the city walls Tate followed interstate 14 east, towards the city of Temple.

Abandoned cars and trucks, metal tombstones of failed migrations, sat huddled in weathered piles on the sides of the interstate.

People were reluctant to travel outside the protective walls of their cities which made these long strips of open road the domain of freight trucks. The big haulers were the backbone of keeping populated areas supplied.

A missed shipment could spell disaster for smaller populations. Many towns would adopt a regular truck driver, treating them with free meals and helping with the maintenance of their tucks.

With derelict cars cleared from the roads, truckers most common obstacle were mobs of Vix. Many drivers fitted the front of their big rigs with a Vix Grill that protected the radiator grill of their truck from clogging up if the driver had to plow though a crowd of them.

A re-enforced steel plow on the front of a speeding, seventy thousand pound freight truck meant these drivers didn't have to slow down for anything. Even a driver in a military, armored truck had to keep their eye on the rearview mirror.

Tate consider how different this environment was to the jungles he'd become accustomed to. He didn't know what to expect once they entered no-man's land, but felt the confidence of sitting inside a four wheeled tank. Distant, spindly forms shimmered through the heat waves which Tate speculated could have been Vix, but the mysterious shape wavered out of sight as the PLAV sped on.

Kaiden guided them around obstacles referenced on her navigation monitor which kept a record from previous patrols of that area including any known Vix hotspots.

Turning off the broad and open I35 Tate slowed when he turned onto W. Central avenue. The intersection ahead was clogged with cars. At the center was an ugly car wreck. The windshield was shattered and twisted metal peeled back from the bumper. Next to it was an abandoned tow truck and a paramedic. A gurney stood empty next to the car.

"Must have happened right out the outbreak," said Wesson, looking out the side window as Tate drove over the sidewalk and through a fast-food parking lot to get around it.

"Looks like the whole place went insane," said Fulton, imagining what the scene must have looked like.

"By the time ambulance arrived the driver was probably dead," said Wesson, as if narrating a scene playing out in her mind's eye. "When the driver turned the crowd didn't understand what was really happening. After it killed a couple of people and those came to life, they got it and ran."

"I wonder how many got away," said Fulton.

"None," said Rosse darkly. "This city ain't walled off which is a sure sign the whole place had more Vix than people before any help showed up."

Fulton looked past the intersection, down the roads until they disappeared from sight. Empty homes and small shops lined them as far as he could see. "All those people."

"The number of dead is so big it stops having any meaning," said Wesson. "Then you see this and it makes it real again."

"I sometimes forget how many we lost," said Monkhouse.

"Who wants to remember?" said Rosse, pointing out the window as they passed a school.

A chainlink fence wrapped around the play yard with rusted

monkey-bars, swings, and slides. The fence bowed outward as dozens of ravenous, child-sized Vix pressed against it. Their stained, weathered clothing hung in limp rags on their rotting frames. They gnawed and pulled at the fence with naked greed flaring in their dead eyes. The thick, armored windows blocked the sounds of their scabrous growls adding a nightmarish cast to the scene.

Kaiden glanced at Tate from the corner of her eye, wondering if the scene would rekindle thoughts of his dead daughter. Tate didn't say anything, but kept his eyes rigidly locked on the road ahead; his expression stony, avoiding the tragic image of the school yard.

"Turn right at the next street," said Kaiden happy to be turning away from the school, "and we're there."

The PLAV rounded the corner bringing a string of train cars into view. To the left was the red tiled roof of the train station. As they got closer Tate was amazed. There were two people casually sitting on a bench in front of the station. He caught himself before saying something when he realized they were statues.

The front of the station was made up of tall, dirty arched windows bordered in brick, and surprisingly, the windows were still intact. The caked dirt made it hard to see inside as Tate pulled up to the front doors.

Across from the train station was a large park dotted with trees and the occasional bench.

"Nothing on this side," confirmed Kaiden, after scanning the park for Vix.

Monkhouse squeezed between the two front seats, bumping Kaiden as he began tapping one of the screens on Kaiden's console.

"Hey, boundaries!" snapped Kaiden.

"Sorry," said Monkhouse. "I just remembered that we have an optics suite up top."

"What about it?"

"We can see if there's any Vix in the train station by using the IR camera on the roof," said Monkhouse as he used the camera's directional joy controller and swirled the camera towards the front of the building.

Kaiden looked at Monkhouse with pained amusement. "That's

brilliant," she said. "I wonder why nobody else thought of using a *thermal* camera to detect... *dead people*."

Monkhouse stopped as Kaiden's words sunk in. "Well, sure. When you put it that way," he muttered. "Do you know if anyone's ever tried?"

Kaiden started to say something, but stopped as she considered the question then swept her hand towards the camera controls, inviting Monkhouse to try it.

Tate watched, halfway expecting Monkhouse to succeed. After a moment Monkhouse sat back grunting as he pushed himself from between the two seats. "I'm not saying it didn't work, but the camera didn't pick up anything inside."

"Everyone out," ordered Tate. "Ota, you're on overwatch."

Ota only nodded as he hefted his sniper rifle. Having embraced the philosophy of Zen at some point in his life, Ota used words sparingly making it easy to forget he was even there. He could be as quick to action, decisive, and deadly as anyone on the team, yet most things didn't phase him. To the utter annoyance of some of his teammates, Ota lived in a bubble of calm serenity, even in the most hectic situations. In the early months of the teams formation a couple of the team tried their best practical jokes to rattle him with zero result. Later, in a candid moment, Ota admitted to Tate he enjoyed the bewilderment he caused his friends. Tate laughed a long time about that, but kept Ota's secret to himself.

"Wesson has security. You all know the drill. Let's go!"

Ota climbed up on the top of the PLAV and settled the stock of his sniper rifle against his shoulder. He began scanning the park for movement while Wesson double-checked the box magazine on her LM-948 squad machine gun.

The rest of the team came out of the PLAV and formed up behind Tate as he took cover behind the brick wall before peeking through the dirt-streaked window.

"I don't see any Vix from here, but it's a big place," said Tate into his radio. "Stand by to enter."

Everyone's readiness went up another notch as Tate tapped the front door's glass with the barrel of his HK-93. Nothing happened for the next few seconds and Tate leaned out of cover to test the latch on the door handle. It didn't move at first and Tate pressed harder on the latch. Suddenly the latch broke free of the crusted dirt and snapped open with loud clack.

Before his mind registered the sound of running feet, the front door glass blew out. Something solid slammed into Tate's outstretched arm, spinning him away from the wall. The charging Vix caught its leg on the doorframe as it flew out of the door and tumbled to the ground on its back.

In an instant it flipped over and came at the team, scuttling on all fours. Tate's right arm was numb with pain and useless. Swinging up his assault rifle with his good hand he tried to point the barrel at the fast moving Vix when it suddenly disintegrated into bone and fragments of rotted flesh as Kaiden, Fulton, Monkhouse and Rosse all opened up at point blank range.

Tate blinked at the near instantaneous transformation from a deadly Vix to a puddle of gunk.

"And stay down!" smirked Monkhouse.

"Movement," said Ota. "Far side of the park."

Rosse hurried over to Tate, examining his arm for breaks or something much worse. "You're okay. There's no blood," he said with relief. "It didn't get you."

Grateful, Tate nodded to Rosse and looked up just in time to see a distant figure running towards them at incredible speed. There was a puff of dust from its head and the figure summersaulted backwards in a twisted heap and didn't move again.

"Nice shot," said Tate, wincing as he opened and closed his battered hand.

"Uh huh," said Ota keeping his eye to the scope of his worn Dragunov sniper rifle.

Ota's rifle barked in three quick successions; his shots echoing into the distance.

"It's going to heat up fast out here," said Tate. "Those shots are going to attract more Vix. Nothing else has come out of the building, so it should be clear. Wesson, set up out here to support Ota. Everyone else is with me."

"Copy," said Wesson and headed for the PLAV.

Tate pulled open the shattered door and looking over the top of his HK 93 he went inside with Fulton, Monkhouse, Kaiden and Rosse behind him.

Light poured in the from the tall, arched windows that lined both sides of the long, narrow building. Dark, wooden pillars lined the middle of the building, reaching up to a attractive coffered ceiling.

Tate quickly studied the dust covered marble floor and was reassured by the single set of footprints of the very dead Vix that there weren't more inside. "Anyone see lockers?" asked Tate.

The others also came up empty.

"There's a set of doors to the left," said Kaiden.

Following Kaiden's prompt Tate saw a set of double doors at the end of the hall. One door was shut, but the other hung crookedly from broken hinges.

"Let go," said Tate.

Weapons up, they fast walked to the doors, peering over the sights of their guns. Behind the broken door, natural light revealed a small room with wooden benches and two walls lined with lockers.

Tate pushed open the working door and entered, frowning as two muted cracks from Ota's gun echoed off the walls. "Wesson, give me a report," said Tate into his radio.

"Just stragglers," said Wesson over the radio. "Light contact so far."

"Copy," replied Tate. "We found the lockers and should be with you soon."

"I got it, Top," said Fulton, pointing to a locker. "1171, right?"

"That's it," said Tate as he fished a folded paper out of his pocket.

Everyone stoped, glancing quickly at the double doors as bursts of machine gun fire thumped the air. Tate hurriedly turned the numbered dial on the locker as he read the combination from his note. The addition of Wesson's light machine gun meant there were more than just a couple of Vix showing up.

"It's getting busy out here," came Wesson over the radio.

Kaiden keyed up her mike. "Status."

"Heavy contact. They showed up from nowhere," said Wesson, trying to keep the strain from her voice. "Status is critical."

"Everyone out," said Tate. "Get safely in the PLAV. I'll radio when I need cover."

"You'll get swarmed," said Monkhouse.

"I said go!" barked Tate.

Monkhouse and Fulton looked at Tate in surprise. Unsure, Fulton looked back the way they'd come and took a reluctant step.

"Nobody leaves," declared Kaiden, freezing a confused Fulton in his steps.

Tate glanced at her hotly.

"This is not up to debate," said Kaiden.

Kaiden didn't melt under Tate's fixed glare and he turned his attention back to the locker. Pushing up the latch, Tate's eyes went wide as he opened the locker revealing several bricks of C4 wired to a small box attached to the door.

Monkhouse grinned appreciatively at the explosives crowding the inside of the locker. "Good thing you remembered to bring the combination. I'll bet you anything he's got all that wired up to a sensor. If the wires break, or it detects any impact everything around here goes poof!"

Tate reached into the locker and took out what looked like a cell phone. He turned it over looking for some indication of what it was or what to do with it.

Long rips of machine gun fire tore his attention from the device.

"Multiple Vix," said Wessons, the stress raising in voice.

Tate shoved the device into his pocket and the team hurried to return to the PLAV as bursts of Wesson's machine gun came rapidly one after another.

Passing through the outside doors Tate didn't need to see the situation because the volume of snarls and growls were enough to know there were a lot of Vix and they were dangerously close.

"They're swarming!" yelled Wesson over the rip of her machine gun.

"Everyone inside the PLAV!" shouted Tate. "Cover fire, but don't sto..."

A shockwave hammered the team making their ears ring as an explosion flashed from the other side of the armored vehicle. Tate staggered as decayed limbs and debris whipped by in every direction from a billowing cloud of smoke and dust. Running to the PLAV, Rosse took a grenade shell out of his pouch and shoved it into the smoking barrel of his grenade launcher attached to his HK 556L.

Operating on instinct, everyone fought through the confusion and piled into the PLAV, slamming the protective doors behind them.

Taking a moment to shake it off, the team panted as beads of sweat streaked their faces and dust swirled though rays of light from the windows.

"What the hell was that?" shouted Monkhouse, his voice ringing in the closed compartment, not that anyone noticed.

"Hey!" objected Wesson. "Stop shouting."

"Am I shouting?" yelled Monkhouse. "I can't hear."

"Damn it, Rosse!" said Tate, trying to get the hum out of his ears.

"Sorry guys," shrugged Rosse. "There was a mob of'em right there. I had to, or they would'a been on us before we got inside."

"Everyone here?" said Tate.

Everyone looked around, ensuring no familiar faces were missing. Shadows passed over the windows and the team felt their seats shift under them. Turning around they looked out the window. Hundreds of Vix surrounded the PLAV in every direction.

"They didn't clean the city out?" said Wesson watching as more Vix filled the ever growing mob.

Tate climbed between the seats into the driver's seat. "Maybe they did and more collected here."

"We need to report this when we get back," said Wesson. "If they came at the city's wall at once..."

"We have to get out of here first," said Tate as the PLAV's engine growled to life.

The Vix reaction was instant and frenzied. The nearest ones attacked the PLAV rocking it on its suspension as the rest pressed in or climbed over to reach the team.

Tate's amazement turned to worry as they piled over each other spilling onto the hood. Even through the armored shell the team could hear the scratch of bone as they scramble onto the roof until sunlight was blocked out from every window.

The chorus of growls, hisses, snarls felt like a physical thing squeezing in on the team making the already tight space feel like it was closing in.

"Top," said Fulton, panic rising in his voice. "What are you waiting for?"

"The hell with this," said Tate putting the PLAV in gear and stomping on the gas. The engine roared as the vehicle lurched forward then stopped.

"What's happening?" said Kaiden as she climbed into the navigators seat.

"I can't get enough traction!" said Tate. "They're packed so heavily around us we can't move. Everyone hang on to something."

Tate threw the PLAV into reverse and hit the gas. It rocked backwards, but only a few feet before jolting to a stop.

Before the Vix could fill the gap in front of the vehicle Tate shoved the gear into *Drive* and put the peddle down. The 8.4 liter, V8 direct-injection engine drove all eight hundred and twenty foot pounds of torque to the massive tires. The chunky treads spun, yanking under bodies, churning flesh and snapping bone until the front of the PLAV rose up on a pile of mangled corpses. The big, armored machine broke free as all four tires clawed up the crush of Vix.

Tate hit his head on the ceiling as the nose of the PLAV plunged over the horde of Vix, tumbling the rest of the team on top of each other. He slammed his foot on the accelerator and they shot forward.

The PLAV charged blindly ahead, its windshield covered with writhing Vix as Tate gripped the wheel with white fingers. Fear screamed in his head, he was about to slam into something. Destroying the engine, killing some of his team and stranding the rest inside this armored coffin, surrounded by Vix, until they starved to death.

Tate forced himself to count off a few more seconds, though it felt like forever. "Hang on!" he shouted, then slammed on the brakes. Someone in the back screamed and bodies tumbled and cursed.

Vix flew off the hood and roof, hitting the ground like rag dolls. In an instant they were on their feet, charging the PLAV.

Glorious light flooded through the windscreen and Tate smashed his boot on the gas. The engine howled, launching the PLAV like a blunt missile. The few Vix that got in the way shattered into pieces as the armored truck pounded over the uneven ground of the park.

Coming off the grass to the street, the gore-slick tires screamed across the asphalt as Tate oversteered the PLAV, sliding it sideways in a cloud of smoking rubber. Bile rose in Tate's throat as the PLAV came off its left tires, threatening to roll. Time stopped as the big armored truck tipped, lingering on the edge of its tires, between escape and disaster. Slowly, at first, Tate could feel the PLAV begin to right itself, then free fall.

Tate's jaw clacked as the PLAV slammed back down, its four tires biting into the road.

Nobody in the PLAV complained that Tate didn't slow down until the town was a smudge in his sideview mirror.

7

STAND OFF

With the overrun husk of Temple behind, and the open prairie ahead, Tate decided to pull off the highway and examine the device he had taken from the locker.

The PLAV had hardly stopped before the team eagerly climbed out, happy to stretch their legs and breathe fresh air.

Tate and Kaiden walked around to the front of the PLAV where Tate turned the palm-sized object over in his hand wondering what to do with it. Its smooth, black surface was featureless giving no clue how to use it.

Kaiden found a spot on the PLAV's bumper, not caked with blood, and leaned against it, watching Tate with a subtle smile. He clenched his jaw seeing her expression from the corner of his eye.

"Okay, what?" said Tate turning on Kaiden. "What?"

"What did I do?" said Kaiden unflustered.

"I know that look," grumbled Tate. "You know what this is, but you're letting me squirm until I ask you."

"That's unfair," said Kaiden. "I know it annoys you when I take over. I was trying to be sensitive."

Tate stared at her, unconvinced, and held out the device to her. "Just make it work."

"I don't think it'll work for me. Put your thumb on the center of it."

Tate followed her instructions and the face of the device came to life, displaying an image of earth. The image zoomed in until coming to a stop over their location and a map of their surroundings appeared.

"I'm impressed," said Kaiden. "Not everyone has this level of tech."

"It's just a GPS," shrugged Tate, unimpressed.

"Give it a second," said Kaiden.

As they watched, the map turned into a real time, birds-eye image. They could see the PLAV and white squares bracketed each team member as they moved around.

"How can Nathan slave real time imaging from satellites?" said Tate.

"We may have underestimated our new friend," said Kaiden meaningfully.

The image zoomed out several miles then stopped adding a new icon on the screen.

"That must be where Nathan is," said Tate. "All right everyone, time to go."

The team loaded back into the PLAV and Tate moved his holster out of the way as he settled into the drivers seat, placing the device on the console so he could see the screen.

He'd been a tier one Delta operator with access to the best military gear and had never seen anything so compact and powerful. *How did she know what it does, or used biometric security?*

He and Kaiden had reached an understanding that he would reign in his suspicions about her, at least outwardly. Even though he trusted her, she kept secret how she had access to advanced gear and intel dossiers. She could have one, or multiple sources including black market, arms dealers, informants, or more worrying a splinter intelligence agency. What was she trading to her sources in return? She knew everything about the Grave Diggers, their clandestine operations against The Ring, secret and classified information about places and people. If their secrets were her currency, what were others doing with that information. There was no knowing whose hands that fall into.

Every time these doubts surfaced Tate would repeat the same arguments he'd wrestled with before and it always came back to the same answer. Trust. He could play the guessing game in an endless string of 'what if' scenarios, or disregard everything but the fact that she had stayed with him through thick and thin, risked her life along side of him on missions, and been good a friend. So, he pushed suspicions back into a box and locked them up, hoping they'd stay there this time.

"Notice I didn't ask how you know about things like that," said Tate, nodding to the device.

"Just a lucky guess," said Kaiden distractedly as she buckled into her seat.

"Yeah," muttered Tate. "That's what I thought."

The PLAVs engine kicked over with a smooth growl and Tate pulled back onto the highway, but his thoughts began down a darker path. His subconscious drew comparisons between Nathan's specialty tech while Tate was lucky to have cable TV. Anger brewed at unfairness of his life in spite of years of honor, character, and self sacrifice while others had life eating out of the palms of their hands.

"In a hurry?" said Kaiden.

"Huh?" asked Tate, coming out of his own thoughts.

"I know we're against the clock," said Kaiden, "but slow down, cowboy."

Tate looked at the console and saw he was pushing 102 miles an hour. The PLAV was a lot of things, but a sports car it wasn't. Warnings on the engine monitor showed the status of the cooling system and oil pressure were in the red and critical. Tate eased off the gas pedal and, one by one, the warnings disappeared.

Kaiden silently looked at Tate, her face empty of any meaning. She knew something was on his mind, but she wasn't going to push him. Coaxing feelings out of someone was for children and moody teens. Tate was a man and, in her opinion, adults decided for themselves if they wanted to express themselves.

Tate didn't always welcome Kaiden's perspective because she

had a knack for hitting a nerve, but he valued her unvarnished honesty, all the same. She saw the complexities within the gray area between the black and white of a situations, but empathy rarely swayed her from expressing the truth which made it hard to hear.

"Am I the only one who feels like we're operating in the stone age?" said Tate, wanting to get it off his chest. "The best we get is decades old equipment. Hell, even our uniforms are out of date."

"Where's this coming from?" said Kaiden.

"Fort Hood. It was like time traveling to the future. And this..." said Tate, pointing to Nathan's device. "Instead of the kind of gear I'd have in Delta I'm fighting with rocks and spears."

Kaiden looked out the window, watching the open prairie drift by. Tate wanted to say more; just vent off the ball of anger he felt in his chest, but knew that would feed into it and he didn't need the distraction clouding his head just before they went into action.

The only sound was the steady hum of the engine until Kaiden turned back to Tate. "You aren't in Delta anymore," she said. "The family you knew is gone."

"Hang on," said Tate. "That's not what I meant."

"Yes you did. Things like that tracker remind you of the life you walked away from. It's gone. You can't go back."

"Thanks," quipped Tate. "That felt good."

"I could lie," said Kaiden.

"Sympathetic isn't your style," said Tate.

"It's not one of my people skills," grinned Kaiden then turned serious. "Do you want little tugs, or should I rip off the bandaid?"

"You mean there's more?" said Tate.

Kaiden only looked at him, waiting.

"I won't like it," sighed Tate.

"Nobody likes honesty," said Kaiden, "It's why I don't have many friends."

"Hell," resigned Tate. "Go on, but just... just give me the quick version."

Kaiden nodded as she brushed her hair out of her eyes. "This war with The Ring is getting serious," she said, "and you're a liability."

Tate hadn't known what he was going to hear, but she was going in a direction he did not expect.

"You're making bad decisions," said Kaiden, "and taking stupid risks. Since Jennie died I think there's times you want to die."

"Her name's Jessie. She's gone. I get it."

Tate fought the restless urge to squirm under Kaiden's long stare. He refused to be the next one to speak, choosing to use the prolonged silence as a weapon.

"She still lives inside of you," said Kaiden.

Tate's breath hitched in his throat her words drove deep inside him.

"If you die," said Kaiden, "that's when you really loser her and she will be gone forever."

Tate could feel himself groping for words as the strength of Kaiden's insight rocked through him. He opened his mouth to speak, but she cut him off.

"But if you're going to die," said Kaiden, "stop dancing around it and just do it. And, have the decency not to suicide by combat risking getting the rest of us killed too."

Kaiden casually turned her attention to the view outside, softly humming to herself.

Tate began to speak then stopped. Started again and stopped. There wasn't anything Tate could say that she was interested in. She'd said what he'd invited her to say leaving Tate to sort through everything he'd heard.

Looking at the satellite map Tate saw a single dirt road coming up that lead to Nathan's location. Turning off the asphalt, the PLAV's tires easily bit into the dry soil, rolling gently on the uneven dirt road. The blue of the sky, above, melted into a dramatic orange where it met the land as the sun began to glide beneath the horizon. Shadows stretched out, creeping over the ground until the soft light of dusk extinguished them.

The rumble of the mighty V8 engine died away as Tate switched the PLAV over to its electric motor. He turned off the headlights and engaged the PLAV's onboard night vision. The NV ultra-sensitive cameras saw everything, transforming the desert into an alien landscape of greens and grays. The hulking armored truck melded into the night with nothing to betray its presence but the soft crunch of its tires.

Several miles later the dirt track rose to a crest and Tate stopped.

Scanning the area ahead with the camera, Kaiden followed the road as it dipped into a small box canyon. At the far side was a one story structure a car parked next to it. She patched her image into the monitor in the back of the PLAV where the rest of the team was sitting.

"Switching to thermal," said Kaiden.

The landscape changed to a grey negative. Cooler objects were darker while the warmer things were lighter, hot was bright white.

Kaiden zoomed the camera in on the car which glowed a pale white.

"It's been there a while," she said. "If the engine was still warm it would be brighter than the rest of the car."

She adjusted the camera until they had a close-up view of the ground in front of the door and then the front door handle.

"What are you looking for," asked Fulton, fascinated with the technology.

"Footprints, handprints," said Kaiden. "That sort of thing."

"No kidd'n," said Rosse, impressed.

"If it's recent enough," said Kaiden, "they can leave a heat signature. Judging by this, nobody's been outside in a couple hours."

She panned the camera over the walls of the building, stopping on a darker patch of wall.

"That's where they are," she said.

"But it's darker," said Fulton. "Wouldn't it be lighter because the people inside warm it up?"

"It's the only room running air conditioning," said Rosse. "Am I right?"

"Yes, you are," said Tate.

"I knew it," grinned Rosse. "The wall's darker because it's cooler than the rest of the house."

"See anything else?" asked Tate.

"If we get closer," said Kaiden.

With almost predatory stealth the PLAV rolled up next to the ranch house. Kaiden trained the roof-top camera on the wall where they suspected Nathan might be and scrolled through the camera settings until she found what she was looking for.

"Come on, baby," she said.

A moment later shadows appeared on the monitor. Vague and indistinct as they were it was clear they were looking at people inside the house.

One shadow was sitting, hunched forward while another shadow was moving back and forth, pacing. Two other shadows stood further away, at an odd angle.

"My guess is that's Nathan," said Tate, pointing to the seated figure. "Those two are leaning."

"On their feet all day," added Kaiden.

"Exactly," said Tate. "They're on guard-duty and nobody sits on guard-duty."

"What about the other one?" asked Fulton.

"Want to field this one, Wesson?" asked Tate.

"It's another guard," said Wesson without hesitation.

"How do you figure," asked Tate.

"The two guards wouldn't let a threat close to them. If it was someone in authority, or their boss, they wouldn't be casually leaning. It's got to be someone equal to them."

"Outstanding, sergeant," smiled Tate, then turned serious. "All right. We have three hostiles, expect them to be armed, in a confined space with our high value target. Ota and I will recon the outside for ways inside then return here."

"You're only going to annoy the boss, Hogan," said the taller of the two guards as they leaned against the far wall.

It had been two days and Hogan was getting cabin fever. Recruited by The Ring shortly after she left the Dutch special forces, Hogan wasn't wired for the stationary demands of being a guard. The constant hum of computer fans and the ion tinge in the air made her crave the openness of the outdoor.

She had been watching Nathan while pacing the room like a restless animal in a zoo. Three times, now, she'd seen strings of numbers scrolling on Nathan's monitor and stop. He'd type something, without comment, and the numbers would begin scrolling again.

"You can't see he's stalling, Pernette?" asked Hogan.

"My job," said Pernette, "is to keep him here; not watch the clock."

"*Eikel*," swore Hogan under her breath. "Bryant, it's your boss," she continued, "you heard him say he wanted quick results."

"You see this?" said Bryant gesturing to his nondescript, dark suit. "We're all wearing the same style because we're supposed to blend into the background. The background doesn't get paid to decide if this guy's stalling. Getting involved is ..."

"Don't say *above your pay grade*," warned Hogan.

Bryant simply shrugged his shoulders and grinned.

"I'm calling the boss and letting him decide what to do."

"You're funeral," said Pernette.

She was right. Nathan was stalling and running out of excuses. The computer had finished calculating the satellite's target area the day before and Tate hadn't appeared.

At the time he sent the message to Tate's sat phone, Nathan was sure he jump at the chance hurting The Ring, but where was he? Doubts began to whisper in his mind that maybe Tate wasn't coming. Or, maybe he was minutes away. Not knowing gnawed at him.

When Walter first brought him to the ranch house Nathan made a mental note of the room in case he had to escape on his own. One door lead back the way he'd come in, through the creepy hallway. The other door led to the bathroom, which surprisingly, had an unbarred window, but after he climbed out where would he go? Open miles of desert lay in every direction. Nathan knew the time to make a decision, wait for Tate, or try to escape on his own was staring him in the face. In his heart he knew that Tate was his only salvation. A salvation he was becoming convinced was not coming.

Nathan had rerun the satellite's reentry calculation twice more and knew it was moments from completing again. Hogan was threatening to call Walter and if she could add to his own suspicions things for Nathan could go very bad.

A new plan occurred to Nathan. It was desperate and dangerous, but he couldn't wait anymore. He had to get himself out of this and his only leverage was if he was the only person who knew the satellite target location. He'd only have a window of a few seconds to act. The moment the mainframe completed its processing he'd have to memorize the satellite vector, target circumference, longitude and latitude then wipe the mainframe memory and crash the system. If he could pull that off before anyone realized he was up to something, he'd be their only source of the information. Leverage.

His thoughts were broken as an arm reached past him and snapped a gate drive into an open port on the computer console.

"What ever this computer is doing," said Hogan, leaning over his shoulder, "I'm making a copy of it."

Nathan's expression hid the urge to yell in frustration, but the distraction cost him dearly as a small window opened on Nathan's screen. The computer recognized the gate drive and requested what action it should take. Before Nathan moved, Hogan mashed the number two key, selecting *Back up file.*

There went Nathan's leverage. His one saving grace was Hogan's impatience. As soon as she pressed that key the mainframe began trying to ram terabytes of data into the gate drive. The multi-layered fiber-optic storage of the gate drive had an incredible transfer rate, but nothing that could keep up with the output the mainframe was throwing at it.

Data began cueing up in a buffer, waiting for the gate drive to catch up. To anyone else the delay was only a few extra seconds, but they were the vital seconds Nathan needed to memorize the information. But, the timing was critical because he'd have to pull out the gate drive before the download completed.

Nathan saw Hogan's face reflected in his monitor as she watched his every movement from over his shoulder. She wasn't going anywhere. His breathing felt rushed and he forced himself to breathe deeply. Stress was his enemy. It would interfere with his focus and short term memory and he desperately needed both to save his life.

Before Nathan recognized the click of the hallway doorknob turning, the three guards were reaching for their pistols. Suddenly the door slammed open and three figures swarmed into the room, shouting, with assault rifles up and ready. Their eyes flashing from dark faces streaked with black and green camo paint.

Bryant and Pernette froze, looking down the barrels of automatic rifles pointed at their faces, but Hogan was faster, her pistol up and standing in an aggressive shooting stance.

"DOWN, DOWN, DOWN!" yelled Tate, Kaiden and Wesson.

"Drop it!" scowled Hogan, aiming squarely at Wesson.

"Put down the gun," cautioned Monkhouse appearing from the bathroom, behind Hogan.

Startled she spun around and backed up, aiming her gun from one intruder to another.

"Drop your weapon," yelled Wesson, aiming at Hogan.

"It's over," said Monkhouse almost soothingly. "Put it down."

Hogan swung her aim, pointing her gun at Monkhouse's face. She was so close he could see her knuckles were white from the death grip on her gun.

"I said drop the damn weapon!" commanded Tate.

Bryant and Pernette, their hands still on the butt of their guns, had recovered from their surprise and were keenly watching for that split-second of advantage to draw and shoot their attackers.

"Lets see who's faster," growled Kaiden, pressing the barrel of her gun against Pernette's eye.

"Drop yours," screamed Hogan. "Last chance!"

Tate's eyes glinted behind the gun site as he braced the stock of his rifle against his shoulder. "Not happening."

Hogan was on the edge of panic, her fingers flexing her grip on her gun, tensing her shoulders to absorb the anticipated recoiled of her gun.

"No, no, no," cautioned Monkhouse. "Don't do that."

She glanced at him in surprise, her face a mask of finality. Her sweat-streaked hair plastered to her cheek, her eyes a mix of fear and anger.

"Let's call it a day, all right?" said Monkhouse, calming his voice. "Everyone's tired. We all just want to go home."

Bryant and Pernette began to tense as they watched Hogan's expression, almost hearing the screaming voices in her head. She whipped her eyes back to Tate, terrified he might have come at her in her seconds of distraction, then back to Monkhouse.

The air felt too thick to breathe, almost solid, slowing time and accentuating the smallest sounds. Monkhouse could sense more than see Tate was about to take the shot and who knows what blood-bath would follow.

"Home," said Monkhouse trying to keep the quiver out of his voice. He tried not looking at Hogan's gun barrel inches from his face. Crouching at the bottom of that dark pit was an unstoppable monster ready to devour his life. "I know I'd like to go home. I bet you'd give anything to be there right now. Soooo."

Light flickered off the satin finish of Hogan's gun from the subtle waver of her grip as Monkhouse's words penetrated her panicked mind.

Momentarily caught up in the stand-off, Nathan had forgotten about the gate drive. His heart slammed in his chest as he saw the progress bar hit ninety eight. Ninety nine. Nathan scrambled out of his chair, pretending to stumble against the computer console and knocked the gate drive loose, where it clattered to the floor.

Startled by the noise, Hogan flinched and pulled the trigger. Monkhouse winced as the hammer snapped down with a muffled thud, and nothing more. He looked up astonished to see Tate standing next to Hogan. His thumb pinned under the hammer of her gun.

Bewildered, Hogan looked up into Tate's grim face. She began to say something, but was cut short as Tate slammed his rifle's buttstock into her head and she crumpled to the floor.

Glaring at Monkhouse, Tate pulled his thumb free and pitched Hogan's gun at his feet.

"Tie her up," growled Tate.

The metal cinch around Monkhouse's chest disappeared and he filled his lungs. Bryant and Pernette dropped their guns and backed up a few steps.

Tate's adrenaline was bleeding off when there was a blur of movement. Before he could react, Nathan picked up Hogan's gun and emptied it into the mainframe computer. The shots cracked loudly as sparks and the smell of burnt plastic spurted out of the machine and the monitors turned to static.

"What ever you're after," announced Nathan, tossing the gun aside, "you're not getting it now."

"Son of a..." sputtered Tate, confused and irritated. "Get him out of here!" ordered Tate. "We'll meet up outside after we bind these three."

Wesson grabbed Nathan by the arm and shoved him toward the door.

Monkhouse pulled a couple of heavy-duty nylon cuffs from his pack and knelt next to Hogan who groaned as she swam back to consciousness. With a *zip* he cinched her wrists behind her back. "This is better than a hole in the head," said Monkhouse. Hogan wasn't listening. Her attention was on the gate drive laying on the floor.

Standing up, Monkhouse was surprised to see Kaiden close in front of him. The way she seemed to appear next to him without making any noise always made him nervous.

"Why didn't you pull the trigger?" asked Kaiden.

"I, uh, I mean," Monkhouse stammered, caught off guard by her question. "I thought I could talk her down."

"You thought?" said Kaiden, intently.

Monkhouse had few interactions with Kaiden, but he thought she was cute, if not a little unapproachable. He may even played with the idea of asking her to have coffee with him, but all of his preconceptions were being obliterated and he could only gape in speechless confusion at her.

"I mean, I could have shot her," fumbled Monkhouse, looking for help from Tate, but he was busy with the prisoners and unaware of the quiet grilling Kaiden was giving him. "But, I didn't get the sense she wanted to shoot."

Kaiden stepped in close to Monkhouse, nearly eye to eye with him. "Your sense?" she hissed. "You let her point a gun at Tate."

The sudden intensity of cold anger radiating from Kaiden's deep brown eyes set off a tingling of fear that spiderwebbed though Monkhouse's body. Any second now, he expected to feel the barrel of her gun under his jaw and she would blow the back of his head off. Instead she pointed to the bound guards on the floor. "Them." Then pointed at Tate, herself and Monkhouse. "Us."

Kaiden was close enough Monkhouse could feel her breath on his face. He nodded quickly, unable to break free of her stare.

Kaiden's expression instantly changed to a bemused smile leaving Monkhouse deeply unsettled. She opened the space between them and patted him, good-naturedly, on the chest making him flinch. "Good talk," she said, sighing lightly.

"I got this one," said Tate, holding Nathan by the arm. "Lets go."

8

IT'S A BIG JUNGLE

Nathan sat, tucked into the troop compartment of the PLAV taking in his surroundings as the rest of the team hid their curiosity about him with varying degrees of success.

"You almost got yourself shot," growled Tate, angrily wiping the camo paint off his face. "What were you thinking picking up that gun?"

"Optics," said Nathan.

Everyone swayed as the PLAV came to a stop.

"Which way?" called Wesson from the driver's seat.

Unsatisfied with his answer, Tate's stared at Nathan, but the connection was reciprocated. Nathan sat back and looked to the front where he saw Kaiden smiling at him from the navigators seat.

"Hello, again," said Nathan. "Pen?"

Kaiden handed him a pen and small notebook between the two front seats. "You look different when you're not strapped to a chair and bleeding."

"I get that a lot," said Nathan as he wrote in the notebook and handed it back to her. "That's my home away from home."

Kaiden took the notebook and typed in the location on the nav-computer. A moment later the directions appeared on Wessons screen. She turned off the dirt track and back onto the paved road.

"I put my people on the line to save you," said Tate. "You better do a lot damn better than *optics*."

Nathan looked meaningfully at the Grave Diggers sitting next to him then back at Tate.

"This is my team," said Tate. "They're cleared for anything you say."

Tate meant what he said and wanted his team to know he trusted them. He was rewarded with a smile from Rosse, then motioned for Nathan to continue.

"Someone sabotaged a satellite that's very important to The Ring," said Nathan. "Now they suspect I had something to do with it and after that computer gave them the information they wanted, I'm pretty sure they were going to kill me."

"And destroying it made it look like you were protecting that information from us," said Tate.

Nathan smiled with a nod as he closed his eyes. "I haven't slept in a couple of days. Lets pick this up when we get to my place."

It had been more than two days since Tate had slept and instead of demanding Nathan to explain what was going on, he sat back and closed his eyes.

Tate was aware of sounds and movement on the distant fringe of his consciousness. He closed his mind to it and let himself slip into the buoyant arms of blackness. A sharper sensation jostled his frame and his numbed senses slowly groped for the source behind the intrusion. Little by little he dragged his way towards the lights and sounds that tugged at him until finally opening his eyes. His herculean effort was rewarded with an image of Rosse standing over him.

"C'mon, top!" said Rosse, shaking Tate's shoulder.

"Yeah, okay," slurred Tate as he gathered his wits. "I'm up. What's going on?"

"We're here," answered Rosse. "That guy's place."

Tate looked around and was surprised to find he and Rosse were the only ones in the PLAV.

"How long have we been here?" asked Tate.

"Not long. He said something about pizza and everybody piled out."

Tate got up and stepped out, bare earth crunching under his boots, into the cool night air. The moon painted the surroundings in light the color of burnished steel. The PLAV squatted next to a weathered farmhouse with a sagging roof. Next to it was an, equally aged, barn with a silo attached. Neither building showed any signs of life.

Something in the way the old house creaked in the breeze made Tate feel melancholy and alone. He looked up at the vast night sky, filled with stars, older than time. How many people, before him, had looked at those same stars. All of them gone now, yet the stars lived on, watching generations come and go. Tate thought about his life, the tragedies and joys, the devastation of losing his little girl; but to the stars, wheeling above, he was a momentary wink, small beyond notice. They were there long before and would be there long after he a forgotten memory. Someday, would those stars look down on a world empty of people, where only the dead walk?

Tate sensed someone near. Next to him, Rosse stood quietly gazing upward.

"You ever think what it would be like to travel space?" asked Tate. "Find civilizations on other planets?"

"Nah," said Rosse. "I don't like foreign food."

"Makes sense," smiled Tate. "Let's get inside."

Thumbing to the barn, Rosse led the way and stopped at the door. Something buzzed and Rosse pulled open the door. Tate was surprised to see that under the rust streaked sheets of corrugated metal, the door was thick steel. It closed behind them with a smooth click of oiled, metal rods locking into place.

They moved down a bare hallway to the only other door and walked into a brightly lit room. Rows of shelves were filled with boxes, electronics and a variety of mechanical and electronic parts. Somewhere ahead he heard voices.

"...Not some 007 gadget that explodes, or shoots killer lasers," said Fulton.

"It's a real radio," said Nathan.

Tate heard the hiss of static as he rounded the last stand of shelves into an open, comfortable room. Nathan was sitting at a desk with Fulton next to him, holding something small and square, and was the source of the static.

"Check it out Top," grinned Fulton. "He gave me a radio."

Tate threw Fulton a distracted thumbs up having spied a stack of pizza boxes, making stomach rumble, and headed straight for them. Savory cheese and pepperoni filled Tate's mouth and he nodded to himself, relishing the flavors.

"*Slam'n my head! Make a wish when I'm dead, when I'm dead, when... I'm... dead.*"

The loud music pumped out of the radio startling Tate and inciting sharp protests from the rest of the team. Fulton pawed at the blaring radio, frantically trying to turn it down. "Sorry!" he said, struggling.

"*That was Chronic Crow, and you're listening to White Hat radio. The enemy of the Deep State. We're watching you. Tonight we're...*"

Nathan dabbed his finger on the radio and the volume instantly dropped. Fulton stood awkwardly under the weight of everyone's stare as Nathan patted him on the shoulder.

"How about I show you the controls, later," offered Nathan. Fulton nodded in agreement.

Still chewing, Tate took the opportunity to see what the room could tell him about Nathan. Against the far wall stood several computer towers with cables snaking up into the ceiling. Central to the room was a large work bench. Circuit boards, meters, and cubby-holes of equipment lined the perimeter of the desk.

"Ready to talk?" asked Nathan, at Tate's shoulder then led the way into another room.

Overhead lights automatically came on revealing a comfortable, tastefully appointed, living area.

Two brown, leather couches bordered a wood and glass coffee table. Rustic wood-slat walls were accented by a black, slate floor. An impressively large TV screen took up most of the farthest wall.

"Do you get a lot of company at your secret lair?" asked Kaiden, noticing the ample seating.

"Better to have it and not need it," said Nathan and sat back on couch, kicking off his shoes.Tate sat across from Nathan as he swallowed down the last of his food, and took in the looks the rest of the team were giving Nathan now that the attention was back on him.

Tate had constantly stressed, to his team, the life, or death, importance of keeping their purpose and knowledge of The Ring absolutely secret, and it was understandable they'd be suspicious of this stranger in their midst. "Before we get started," said Tate, looking around at his team, "I'll fill in the blanks about Nathan and how our interests are connected."

He told them how he and Nathan had crossed paths, crediting Nathan with revealing The Ring's ultimate goal of taking over the government, and Nathan's offer to provide intel if Tate and Kaiden rescued him from being tortured to death.

"And I thought we'd never hear from you again," said Kaiden.

"You sound disappointed," said Nathan with a grin.

"No," smiled Kaiden, "but the day is young."

Tate coughed, breaking into the exchange, getting Nathan's attention. "Lets get on topic," he said, "your message said you had info that could destroy The Ring."

"When I sent that message," said Nathan, "I was rushed for time. There were a couple of details I left out."

The overhead light cast a shadow on Tate's face as he leaned forward, highlighting his scowl. "What details?"

"He doesn't have the information," said Kaiden.

Tate kept his eyes fixed on Nathan, taking his time as he drew a long breath. "I took a huge risk to come here and it could come back to bite me. After the day I've had my good nature is in short damn supply, so what you say in the next few minutes had better be very important."

Nathan's expression gave nothing away as he placidly met Tate's stare. "All right," sighed Nathan, sitting up. "Some time ago The Ring hired me to piggy back their communications onto a satellite, named Vulcan 4. They chose it because it uses an encrypted microwave frequencies, which would safeguard their own communications from prying eyes."

"The entire country is criss-crossed with fibre-optics," said Monkhouse, unable to resist jumping in. "It doesn't make sense they'd use a satellite."

"It does if The Ring's connected to someone overseas," said Tate.

Nathan's subtle nod confirmed Tate's statement.

"I figured we were punching above our weight, before," said Rosse, "but if these clowns are getting help from another country, I mean, look at us. We can hardly put a dent in em."

Expressions around the room turned somber as the magnitude of their enemy hit home. Tate wanted to say something to bolster their spirits, but he was struggling under this unexpected revelation, too.

"Before everyone starts singing dirges," said Kaiden, "why don't you finish what were you saying." She looked at Nathan and twirled her finger in the air for him to get on with his story.

"Whoever picked that satellite didn't do their homework," said Nathan. "Vulcan 4 belongs to the NSA and those guys take the concept of Big Brother to a psychotic level. They record every phone call, email and text everyone makes."

"You mean, like, *everyone*, everyone?" asked Fulton. "That's like, I don't know, like, millions of emails, and calls and stuff.

"Everyone, everyone," confirmed Nathan. "And it's closer to billions, but the real irony, and what The Ring just found out, is that Vulcan 4 also records its own transmissions. It doesn't have the onboard storage capacity to record the contents of each transmission; those are archived one of a dozen server farms around the country. But, the satellite carries an onboard database key of every transmission, date, time, origin and destination, including keywords and other markers."

"Anyone with that database key," said Kaiden, "could review and access every communication The Ring's sent and received."

"Including operational names, dates, contacts," said Tate as he wondered at the possibilities.

"Every plan," added Wesson.

"It gets better," said Nathan. "Two days ago, somebody accessed Vulcan 4's navigation systems and sent it on a course back to earth."

Tate could only chuckle at the chaos that must have erupted when The Ring heard about that. "Was that you?" he asked.

"No," said Nathan, "but they suspect me."

"That would have been enough reason for them to kill you. Instead they lock you up with a mainframe?" said Kaiden thoughtfully. "They wanted you to put it back in orbit."

"Very good," smiled Nathan. "Then what?"

Wesson, sitting across from Tate, looked at him questionably at the interplay between Nathan and Kaiden. Tate put his head in his hands with a sigh.

"The rest is simple," said Kaiden. "Whoever brought it down knew where Vulcan 4 would crash. You changed its reentry and were using the mainframe to calculate the new location."

"Now it makes sense why you shot up the computer," said Tate, "The guards will say you sabotaged us from getting the information and look like a hero. All of that is great, but do you know where it's coming down?"

"Yes," said Nathan.

"Did you stop the back-up in time?" asked Kaiden.

Nathan didn't have an answer. If he had stopped the backup, all well and good, but if he hadn't...

Puzzled, Tate looked over at Kaiden. "What back up?"

"When we charged in," said Kaiden, "I saw him knock a gate drive out of the mainframe. He wouldn't have done that if it wasn't backing up the crash site location. Did you stop it?"

"I can't be sure," said Nathan firmly. In the confusion of Tate and the Grave Diggers appearing with guns drawn, Nathan had taken his eyes off the monitor. It was only for a second, but could that vital data been saved in that moment? He didn't know. Realizing he'd lost track of the download, he slapped at the gate drive, not sparing the time it would have taken to check the status first.

Did the mainframe finish its calculation in that time? Inwardly, Nathan admitted it was possible. But, did he think it was likely? *No. Possibly a 2% chance*, he thought. "I can't give absolutes. There's a very small chance the back up finished before I knocked it out."

Tate wearily got to his feet, stretching the kink out of his back as he frowned in thought. The others watched him pace the short space behind the couch, as he sorted out his thoughts until he faced the group, putting his hands on his hips.

"We still hold the advantage," said Tate. "Worst case scenario, The Ring knows where Vulcan 4 will come down, but they believe Nathan doesn't. They won't expect any opposition and they don't want a lot of people knowing about their downed satellite. They'll send a small team. That will reduce the risk of someone getting clever and making off with the database key."

"There's one more thing," said Nathan.

"Aw crap," blurted Rosse. "I heard just about all the bad news I need for one day."

Everyone looked at Rosse and he instantly regretted not keeping his thoughts to himself. "What?" he said defensively. "Am I wrong cause I want things to be easy for once?"

"It's all right, Rosse," said Tate with a smile. "I feel the same way. What else have you got, Nathan?"

"The mainframe could only narrow down the target site to seventy five square miles," said Nathan, "but," he added quickly, "when Vulcan 4 lands it will trigger a transponder signal. I know the frequency. The Ring doesn't."

"Their team could spend weeks running a typical search grid," said Wesson. "The transponder will point us directly to the satellite,"

"He could'a led with that," chuffed Rosse. "This mission's sounding a lot better now."

"How much time do we have before it comes down?" asked Tate.

Nathan looked at his watch, doing a quick calculation in his head. "Fifty three hours from now."

"I, uh, couldn't help noticing," said Monkhouse, "those shelves full of gear, we passed. Any chance you have something able to receive and locate the satellite?"

"Vulcan 4 is an NSA bird," said Kaiden. "Its transponder will be encrypted."

Nathan looked at Kaiden with a sardonic raise of his eyebrows.

"But...," she said, "you already knew that."

"I'll put something together to help you track it," said Nathan, turning back to Tate. "After that, it's up to you and your team."

"Let's get it done," said Tate.

———————————

Tate walked into the gloom of the workroom as Nathan hunched over a pool of light on his desk.

He didn't look up as Tate peered over his shoulder at the splay of electronics. The tracker was laid open like a dissected alien with wires stringing out to a confusing array of equipment.

"Impressive," said Tate.

"Most of this is standard stuff," said Nathan. "Function and protocol analyzers. I'm boosting the signal generator for longer range."

"I meant that you know how to do this."

Nathan smiled, but kept his attention on his work.

"After I freed you from San Roman," said Tate, "I had my doubts I'd hear from you again."

"That cartel boss had psycho written all over him. You took a big risk for me. That's not something you see in my world."

"When you said you'd let me know if you got any good intel on The Ring I didn't expect to see a message on my sat-phone," said Tate.

"It seemed the quickest way to reach you," shrugged Nathan.

Tate watched Nathan study a scrawl of alpha-numeric characters on one of several screens.

"And all you had was my name," said Tate.

Nathan said nothing as he kept his focus on the tiny components of the tracker, but Tate saw a Nathan's eyebrow arch.

"Even as an outsider," said Tate, "I can appreciate not everyone could have hacked my phone. Isolating a satellite's transponder codes. Bypassing NSA security and getting past my sat-phone encryption."

"You forgot lifting your fingerprint to program the biometric lock my GPS," added Nathan. "That wasn't easy."

"Yeah. I didn't see that coming," chuckled Tate.

Tate pulled over a nearby chair, its legs screeching across the floor. Nathan resisted the urge to lean away as Tate sat down uncomfortably close to him. He silently watched Nathan work, indifferent to his claustrophobic presence.

Nathan shot Tate a meaningful look as the impulse to squirm eroded his concentration.

"Uncomfortable?" asked Tate.

"Was I obvious?"

"It's human nature," said Tate. "Having someone too close makes people instinctively feel vulnerable. There's no time to react to an attack." Tate looked squarely at Nathan. "It's like how you could find me; hack my phone; get my fingerprints. It makes me feel vulnerable. That's a problem," said Tate, gravely. "For *both* of us."

Nathan stopped his work on the tracker and looked at Tate with sigh. "Is there a threat implied?"

"I don't imply," said Tate. "Besides," he said as he shifted his chair back giving Nathan room to breathe, "you and I are on the same side. In order to fix our problem you and me are going to devote the next few minutes to improving my level of trust in you starting with who you really are and where you learned your skills."

"I'm disappointed, sergeant major," said Nathan. "Enhanced interrogation doesn't seem your style."

"It's not me you have to worry about," said Tate as he leaned forward. "I'll put it in perspective. Twice I've stood between you and a bullet in the head. The next bullet is inevitable. If you don't get me to trust you, well..." Tate gently tapped Nathan on the forehead, "I may not be there to stop it."

The reality of Tate's words struck Nathan so hard his mouth almost fell open. Until this moment he had glossed over the real possibility he'd be rotting in the desert with the back of his head blown off if Tate hadn't rescued him. Before that, Tate had risked his life saving him from torture and death at the hands of the psycho, cartel boss, San Roman.

He had no intentions of betraying Tate, but in his world you never said never. Still, as Tate had reminded him, anonymity wasn't the safeguard it used to be. In fact, bleeding the life out of The Ring would require him to get a lot closer.

Nathan's shoulders slumped as he resigned himself to tell Tate what he wanted. Perceiving a change in Nathan, Tate relaxed and leaned back in his chair, folding his arms across his chest.

"Lets start at the beginning," said Tate.

9

LOAD OUT

Monkhouse stood under the lit awning attached to the fuselage of the salvaged helicopter and his pride and joy, the Moth. Insects circled the bright work lights with an angry buzz. Monkhouse ignored the errant bug in his face standing with his feet planted and arms folded across his chest, doing his best to protect his beloved Moth from the demands of Jack Tate. "She'll never make it," declared Monkhouse. "I spent weeks patching her up after the last mission. We lost the nose turret in the bay and I don't know if I can ever jury-rig another."

Tate couldn't decide if he wanted to laugh, or yell. From the moment they'd liberated the junked helicopter from a murdering band of scavengers, Monkhouse had adopted it as his own, staunchly protecting it from harm. Anytime Tate had even looked at it Monkhouse would begin to grumble.

"This?" said Tate pointing to Monkhouse and then himself, "I don't have time for. We're leaving in four hours and that chopper's going to take us."

"She doesn't have the range. It's nearly six hundred nautical miles. She doesn't carry that kind of fuel capacity."

"I covered this in the briefing," said Tate, feeing himself beginning to bristle. "There's a forward base we can refuel at."

Monkhouse opened his mouth, but Tate stopped him before he could speak.

"If that doesn't fly, it goes to the scrap yard, or worse."

"Worse?"

"I'll have Rosse sell it on the blackmarket," said Tate.

Monkhouse blanched. "You wouldn't do that. I mean... look at her."

"If I wanted to stare at something big and useless," said Tate, "I'd watch TV. You're going to have that chopper ready to go in," Tate looked at his watch, "three hours and fifty six minutes."

"Or else, what?" said Monkhouse, hurriedly softening his question, and instantly regretting challenging Tate's order.

Tate took a step closer, invading Monkhouse's personal space and leaned in. "Do I look like someone who needs to explain how ugly, 'or else' will be?"

"Sorry, Top," said Monkhouse. "That was out of line. She'll be ready."

"I'm happy to hear it," said Tate as he held Monkhouse in his unblinking stare for a moment longer. He quickly turned and walked away before he couldn't keep a grin from cracking his stoney expression. It was hard for Tate to be offended when Monkhouse turned into such a mother hen.

"Ahhhhrooooooooo, hahahaha! This is Revolution Terry, bringing you White Hat Radio where the truth never dies. I expose the *real* news the black hats don't want you to know."

"Black hats?" said Rosse. "Are ya kidding me?"

The team was on the last leg of their four and a half hour flight to the center of where Vulcan 4 was supposed to come down.

The Moth's crew bay was directly under the engines and the headsets everyone wore couldn't block out its constant noise.

Fulton was eager to listen to his new radio, and Tate had held off letting him, to save the rest of the team from enduring a different, but equally unpleasant noise. Not everyone shared Fulton's tastes. But, they were close to their infiltration point, so Tate let him do it.

There was a short crackle as Fulton had plugged his radio into his headset and it was oldies music and conspiracy theories ever since.

"Black Hats are no joke," said Fulton. "They're part of the deep state. Did you hear about that train wreck last month? That was no accident."

"Aw crap, here we go," scoffed Rosse.

"One of the people on that train was this girl, Spy Cat," said Fulton, with growing enthusiasm.

"Spy Cat?" laughed Rosse.

"Nobody uses their real names," said Fulton. "It's way too dangerous. Anyway, she discovered coded messages in commercials for a shoe store. She wrote all about it. It's one of the ways the deep state sends messages."

"A shoe store offed this girl," said Rosse. "Are you hearing yourself?"

"It's true!" said Fulton.

"How does this radio guy..."

"Revolution Terry."

"Whatever, how's he know about any of this?" asked Rosse.

"People who know things about the Deep State, like Spy Cat, heard his show. They all started to network with each other," said Fulton.

"The Tin Foil Hat club?" chuckled Rosse.

"You can laugh, but there's a lot of people who listen to Terry. Now that they're talking to each other, we're starting to see the bigger picture of what's going on. Terry's probably got a bigger spy network than the CIA."

"How long have you been listening to this crap?" asked Rosse.

"A while," said Fulton. "A guy in my old squad had a radio. Then I transferred here."

Tate glanced over his shoulder at Kaiden, in the pilots seat, and saw a grin curling the corner of her mouth. He wondered what she thought about Fulton's belief in these conspiracy theories.

"What's our ETA?" asked Tate.

Kaiden switched her multifunctional display to the flight management system and scanned the data on her screen. The flight control panel looked like it had been picked over by scavengers. Wires hung out of holes in the panel where instruments and controls were missing. Monkhouse had enlisted one of the helicopter mechanics, on base, to help make the Moth airworthy, but it still had a long way to go. A piece of duct tape covered one of the holes. Someone had drawn a button on it and written "Press button in case of engine fire."

"The good news is," said Kaiden, "we'll be there in five minutes."

"What's the bad news?" asked Tate.

"We'll be there in five minutes," said Kaiden.

"Something tells me you don't like this mission," said Tate.

"What's not to like?" said Monkhouse. "We're landing in the middle of a bale of hay seventy five square miles wide, populated with, who knows, how many Vix while looking for a needle. That's a good time in anyone's book."

Kaiden found a wide clearing that would easily accommodate the Moth. "Eyes open. Going to whisky, delta."

Landing in the wild was insanely risky. Especially areas of dense vegetation because it could be hiding any number of Vix. It became common practice to make noise, and draw them into the open before setting down. The tactic was aptly referred to as *waking the dead*, or whisky, delta.

Wesson swung her machine gun out of the port door and Rosse aimed out of the starboard door as Kaiden came down low and circled above the tree tops.

The trees thrashed wildly under the Moth's beating prop-wash. Clouds of dust and leaves kicked up and an unseen monkey screeched in panic, diving to the jungle floor and bolting for the safety.

Kaiden circled a few times, but with no sign of Vix she brought the Moth down into a clearing. Pulling back on the stick she flared the helicopter, quickly slowing down until the skids bumped onto the ground.

As the rotors spun, all guns pointed out both sides of the Moth, a final precaution should any Vix break out of the distant tree line and charge them.

"Okay, shut it down," said Tate, after they'd waited a couple of minutes.

The whine of the helicopter's engines dropped in pitch as Kaiden flipped a row of switches, shutting them off.

Everyone climbed out of the Moth's cramped bay, glad to stretch their legs.

Wesson got the team to work, setting up a temporary camp and reported back to Tate.

"Thank's Wesson," said Tate.

"When's the satellite due?"

"According to Nathan, sometime today."

"What are we doing with the database after we get it?"

"The first thing is getting past the encryption," said Tate.

"Doesn't the database also have NSA information?"

Tate tilted his boonie hat forward, shading his eyes as he admired the rich, blue of the sky. "Yes."

"Can she break the encryption?" asked Wesson with a nod at Kaiden, who was filling out the flight log in the Moth's cockpit.

"I didn't ask, but I figure since she hasn't volunteered by now, that would be a *no*."

"I was thinking about what Nathan said. Vulcan 4 was the only communication pipeline for American intelligence agencies to talk to their assets in southern Europe. Some of that is probably 'above top secret'," said Wesson.

"I understand where you're going with this," said Tate, "I don't know who I'm giving the database."

This question had been looping through Tate's mind, and he was no closer to a decision. Vulcan 4's database was a backdoor key to untold amounts of intelligence agency secrets. Black ops movements, operational reports from deep cover operatives, bribes of money, drugs, or weapons to pay for information, etc., and in the wrong hands, that information could inflict incalculable damage. But, in that same box was the information that could be used to expose The Ring. Tate asked himself what would he lay on the sacrificial alter in payment for wreaking havoc on The Ring. He stopped himself before he finished the thought, uncomfortable with the answer taking shape in his mind.

Clearing his throat, he changed the subject. "Vulcan 4 could come down anytime after sixteen hundred hours. Set up a two man security detail and rotate them every four hours. Have them check the tracker once an hour."

"Copy that," said Wesson. "What's the tracker's range?"

"Maybe two klicks. If we don't get a hit on by morning, we'll start a patrol from here and spiral out until we get a signal.

The crest of the ridge was broken as a pack of feral dogs raced over the top. From three hundred yards away, heat waves rippled their images, but it was clear enough to see though the rifle scope that one of them had an arm clamped in its jaws. The pack was skittish and glanced nervously over their shoulders. They ran a short distance down the hill and stopped, turning around.

The sniper could see their hackles raise and dropped their heads in silent growls. A moment later a Vix came stumbling over the crest. One arm was missing and the front of its shirt hanging in shreds. A jagged hole had been chewed open in its chest and part of its ribcage was missing.

The Vix turned its head left and right as the dogs began to fan out, then it charged towards the middle of the pack. The dogs crouched, ready to spring.

The sniper observed the blades of grass near the unfolding drama, judging the direction and strength of the breeze. His finger rested, whisper soft, on the trigger as he braced the stock of the rifle against his shoulder. The crosshairs floated closer to the Vix until the intersecting, fine lines rested above and to the left of the Vix's head. Exhaling smoothly, the sniper pressed his finger against the ridged trigger. At two ounces of pressure the trigger released with a crips snap. The silencer on the end of the barrel coughed sharply as the bullet took flight, traveling at three thousand feet per second.

The recoil briefly jostled the snipers view, but he quickly re-acquired his target just as the bullet hit home. A chunk of skull flew off the Vix in a puff of mist and the startled dogs leapt back. The Vix's head snapped back from the impact then popped up just as quickly. A moment later it toppled forward. Confused, the dogs turned, and ran down the hill with the Vix rag dolling behind them, disappearing from view.

No sooner had he lost sight of the Vix the sniper caught movement at the edge of his lens from the dense woods, where he'd just shot the Vix. Fixing his scope on the area, he watched as seven people emerged, in single file.

With Rosse in the lead, they left the shade of the jungle along the spine of the ridge. Tate instantly felt the sun's heat hit him and he adjusted his boonie hat, shading his eyes as he took in the surrounding area.

A distant rumble got everyones attention as dark clouds crowded the horizon.

"Looks like rain," said Fulton.

"Ya think?" said Rosse. "Just what we need. More steam, cause, you know, the jungle doesn't suck enough."

For the past four hours they'd traveled a few miles in each direction from their camp with not so much as a blip on the tracker. Everyone knew bad weather was going to make moving through the jungle harder.

"Ten minutes rest," called Tate. "Wesson, see me after they do a water check."

"Everyone, double check your packs," directed Wesson. "Make sure they're closed up tight and dry."

"That ain't gonna help," groused Rosse. "My pack's got more holes than my underwear."

"Did you see the packs they had at the PX?" asked Fulton. "Why didn't you get one of those?"

Rosse at Fulton for a moment. "What are ya, my mother?"

Wesson and Kaiden joined up with Tate as he took out his map. "I think we're spinning our wheels," he said. "I say we head back to the Moth and fly a spiral pattern." Tate drew his finger in a circle on the map.

"Do we have enough fuel for that," asked Wesson, "and still make it back?"

"That won't be an issue if that storm hits us," said Kaiden. "We'll be grounded."

The sniper's crosshairs moved from one team member to the next, his years of experience intuitively sizing them up and reading their body language. Settling his crosshairs on Tate, the sniper saw a typical second-hand militia type. From his weathered boonie hat and outdated assault rifle to the mismatched camos and paunch belly.

"These guys all buy from the same catalogue?" said the sniper to himself.

But there was something in the man's bearing that made the sniper give him a second look. Years of experience had taught him, he could learn a lot from the little things. The man didn't point when he gave orders; a sign of respect and confidence in his people. After a brief look at his surroundings, the man quickly identified where a threat would most likely come from and positioned his people accordingly. The sniper moved his view down to the man's feet. When standing still he didn't slouch or lean his weight on one foot, but kept it even between both feet making it easier to move in any direction if he had to avoid a quickly. The sniper moved his crosshairs back up the man's body thinking there was more to this man than met the eye when his breath froze in his lungs. The man was looking right at him through a pair of binoculars.

The sniper had set up his position amid clumps of tall grass. To counter the natural ability of humans to recognize the features of a face, the sniper had placed blades of grass into the netting that hung from the front of his hat helping him to blend into the natural patterns of the grass, yet the man continued to look his way.

The sniper forced himself to breathe soft and steady as he moved his finger to the rifle's trigger with glacial speed. He'd been careful not to upset the organic shape of the grass when he'd threaded the barrel of his rifle through it. If anything would betray his *hide* would be the scope. The wind only had to blow the wrong way to part the grass for an instant and expose the dark, round shape of his sniper's lens.

The binoculars could deflect the bullet, so the sniper set the crosshairs on the man's center mass. The cavitation, or shock wave, caused by the bullet would pulverize his heart and lungs. The body would drop before the group heard the shot giving the sniper time to get more kills before the rest of them scattered.

All sense of time disappeared. Heat, sweat, the small pebble that was digging into his thigh for the last hour all faded into nothingness. All that existed was the sniper's breathing and every minute movement the distant man made.

And then the spell was broken. The man swiveled his binoculars, looking at another hill, then lowered them. The sniper eased his finger off the trigger and let his body relax. The sniper almost laughed as he watched the man pull a roll of toilet paper out of his pack and disappear back into the woods they'd first come from. What amused him wasn't the toilet paper, but the tomahawk hanging from the man's belt.

"Guy thinks he's Daniel Boone."

"What'd you say?"

"Nothing, Andy" said the sniper as he heard the soft crunch of footsteps approach. "Just checking out some locals."

Andy grunted as he squatted next to the sniper and fished out a compact monocular from his shirt pocket. Thunder smacked the air and the smell of ozone was becoming stronger.

"I don't get why these peasants want to live in this armpit of the world?" said Andy, as he scanned the distant group.

"Hey man," said the shooter, "my grandparents were born in this country."

"Well," scoffed Andy, "sucks to be them."

The sniper took his eye off the scope, looking darkly at the newcomer. "We hardly been on this op, hombre, and I'm already fed up with you."

"Take it easy, Fernandez," chuckled Andy. "I'm just breaking up the boredom for you."

"I don't need you doing anything for me," said Fernandez as he put his eye behind the scope.

"Are they a problem?" asked Andy as he squinted into the distance.

"No," said Fernandez. "They're small time locals. They'd piss themselves if they knew we were here."

Tate blinked his eyes as he adjusted to the relative gloom of the dense jungle. He stopped near a tree whose trunk was crowded with bushy ferns. Slivers of dust filled light did little to define the jumble of shapes surrounding Tate as he sat down on a thick root.

"Was I right?" asked Tate.

"Yes," said Ota.

Tate saw two eyes appear out of the shadows between the tree and ferns. If not for that Ota would have been completely invisible. With the barest rustle, Ota stepped out of his snipers hide and sat next to Tate while cradling his Dragunov.

"The sniper is behind the mound of tall grass, third from the left," said Ota. "Another one showed up just as you came here."

Tate took off his boonie hat and mopped the sweat off his forehead with a sigh. "Could you make out any details?"

"One's a male. The shooter, unknown," said Ota easily. "The sniper was well hidden and the new guy was obscured by the brush."

"The good news is the sniper didn't shoot us on sight. Maybe they're locals, or a hunting party. We'll know more if they follow us. For now, at least, I don't think they're a threat."

"Because they didn't shoot you?" asked Ota. "A lion doesn't kill when its stomach is full, but it's no less dangerous."

Tate put his boonie hat back on as he stood up. "Most people just say, 'I think you're wrong'," said Tate.

Ota only shrugged his shoulders and smiled.

"Yeah, I get it," scoffed Tate. "You like not being most people."

The team could hear the rain before it hit. A distant, hiss that quickly grew louder like a hundred jets of steam. Wesson instinctively hunched her shoulders beneath her poncho in anticipation of the downpour seconds before it swept over them.

In minutes the ground was saturated creating pools of water with rivulets criss-crossing the ground. Thick, sticky mud caked over their boots weighing down each step until their legs were burning with exertion.

They were nearing the bottom of a hill which opened to a flat plane, several feet wide, that snaked its way across their path.

"Rosse," called out Wesson. "hold up."

Happy for the reprieve, Rosse stopped, resting his hands on his knees as he caught a breather.

"Wesson?" asked Tate, joining them at the front of the line.

"That's an arroyo just ahead," said Wesson, pulling back the hood of her poncho.

It didn't look special to Tate, but Wesson could track and read terrain better than anyone he'd known in special forces.

"What's a yo-yo," asked Rosse.

The rain plastered Wesson's brown hair to her head and streamed off her face as she tilted her head for a moment then seemed to nod to herself. "If we're crossing," said Wesson, "we have to go fast."

"Everyone get going, now!" shouted Tate.

Rosse looked puzzled but took off across the plane with the rest of the team close behind. Wesson led them up a small rise where she stopped, looking back.

"Hear it now?" said Wesson.

Tate pulled back the hood of his poncho, listening. Inside the sizzle of the rain, he heard the a low rumble growing louder.

"Good call," said Tate with a smile.

Suddenly the arroyo disappeared under a surge of muddy water. The flash flood churned and frothed with surprising power, carrying heavy branches and uprooted plants in its wake.

"Don't you love nature?" asked Monkhouse.

"Give me a prison riot any day," grumped Rosse.

The storm wasn't improving and they were forced to turn around as soon as they found a safe place to cross the water.

Weighing their options, Tate knew taking the Moth was out of the question, now. The wind had picked up and was driving the rain down hard. They could hunker down and wait out the storm, but if this wasn't a typical blow there was no telling how long it would last. What he really wanted was to get Nathan on the sat-phone and chew him up. He said the satellite's reentry time was only an estimate and could be off by several hours. *It's been more than several hours*, thought Tate. The team was only provisioned for a few days and he didn't like the idea of rationing food against the demands the jungle puts on the body.

His thoughts were broken as the ground lit up in a brilliant, bolt of lightening, but the light didn't disappear.

"Wow!" exclaimed Fulton, looking up.

The clouds above them pulsed and glowed with an unnatural light that radiated from within. As they all watched, a bright, fiery streak of light broke from the clouds slashing a trail sparks behind it.

"That's the satellite!" said Fulton.

"It ain't the tooth fairy," quipped Rosse.

"Who needs this," said Monkhouse holding Nathan's tracker, "when you have a big, flaming 'X' marks the spot. Finding that database just got a lot easier."

As they watched, the ball of light flared sharply and split into two bright, incandescent fingers falling away in different directions until both were lost behind the canopy of trees.

"You were saying?" said Rosse.

"What happened?" asked Fulton.

"The satellite," sighed Kaiden "just became plural."

After roughing out separate search grids for the two pieces of the satellite, Tate split teams, Rosse and Monkhouse would go with him and Wesson took Fulton and Ota.

For reasons of her own, which she rarely shared, Kaiden chose to go with Wesson. Tate shrugged his shoulders, avoiding the futility of trying to understand Kaiden.

Wesson's destination was closer and Tate had instructed her to join up with him after she located her half of the satellite.

The rain hadn't let up and, in fact, had gotten heavier, driving even the most hearty wildlife into shelter.

Tate didn't like splitting up the team, especially when, somewhere in the jungle, were two the men he'd spotted, earlier. Neither he, or Ota had seen them since, which he hoped was a good sign.

The wind swept up the side of the low hill they were cresting blowing rain in their faces. Squinting against the pelting drops, Tate saw a dark smudge raising up in the distance.

"What's that?" asked Monkhouse. "Smoke?"

Tate took a plastic covered map out of his pocket, fighting the wind as it snapped and pulled in his hands. "There's a small village over there," said Tate. "Looks like our part of Vulcan 4 crashed there and started a fire."

"That satellite's got an entire jungle to crash into," chuckled Monkhouse, "and it smashes into the only village for miles around. I guess if there isn't a trailer park to wipe out, the next best thing is a village."

Forty minutes later they stopped inside a thicket of trees. From there Tate, Monkhouse and Rosse scanned what they could see of the small village. Rural buildings sprawled out, in an open plain, from left to right. Rusted, tin roofs sat on white, blue and amber painted cinder block homes of different sizes and configuration.

The cluster of homes straddled a single, hard packed, dirt road that continued out into the jungle on either end of the village. Wisps of smoke curled up through the rain from somewhere among a huddle of buildings near the center of the village, but there were no signs of flames, or people.

"We go in," said Tate. "Eyes open and call out if you have a contact."

Any chance of hearing the telltale growl of a Vix was drowned out in the downpour and when the wind gusted, the rain came down in such thick sheets it was like looking through fog. You wouldn't see a Vix until it was about to grab you.

"Does it matter that I don't wanna go in there?" asked Rosse as he pushed a 40mm shell in the grenade launcher of his HK 556L.

"Nope," said Tate.

"How about if I don't like it either," said Monkhouse, who was feeling his nerves begin to tingle. There was a lot to be said traveling in the company of six armed teammates, but his confidence had been draining away soon after the team split up.

"I don't see the problem," said Tate. "Almost every village we've been to we've been ambushed by the locals, or attacked by flesh eating nightmares from Hell."

"You don't see a problem with that?" asked Monkhouse incredulously.

"No," grinned Tate. Now that you know what's coming, you won't be surprised when it happens."

10

IT JUST GOT WORSE

The wind swept rain blew in a mix of fat, heavy drops and fine mist, obscuring sight and sound, both which Tate depended on to detect danger *before* it was on him. And it could come from any direction.

Adrenaline trickled through his body, urging Tate's breathing and heart rate to race faster. His mouth felt dry and his mind began jumping from thought to thought.

Tate recognized what was happening and fought it back. He forced his mind to ignore the buzzing hum coursing through his body. Using a technique he'd learned in the Army Rangers, he forced himself to divide his breathing into four second actions. Inhale, hold, exhale, hold and repeat. Instantly, he could feel the constriction in his chest loosen up and his breathing came easier.

Are you done, you frecken lightweight? All right. Lets do this.

Leaving his concealment behind, he angled his approach to the village away from the entrance and headed into a cluster of dense trees and plants that hugged a string of buildings near the middle-edge of the village.

A few feet into the trees he signaled everyone to stop. They all crouched as Tate watched and waited. Everything around them was moving, making it impossible to tell if the source was the wind or something much more dangerous.

Monkhouse was battling his mounting anxiety as he tried to look in every direction at once, convinced, in the next second, a Vix would charge the moment he looked away. He almost jumped when Rosse elbowed him, signaling they were moving out.

Tate repeated the start and stop movement as the dense foliage squeezed between two homes, sharply ending at the edge of the main road. The rain drummed against the nearby corrugated, sheet metal roofs drowning out all other sound. Water pooled over the toes of their boots as the rain came off the roofs in an endless waterfall.

There was something. A sound out of rhythm with the storm. Tate tilted his head, listening until he caught it. The sound came and went from the empty window above Rosse's head. Tate held his palm towards his men, pointed to himself and then the window. Cautiously, he raised up to peer through the window. He could smell it before his eyes adjusted to the dark. The pungent, feted stench of rotted meat told him more than his sight.

A shadow moved within the gloom and bumped into a table. With a rattling hiss, the shadow clawed at the table a few seconds, then went still. A moment later the scene repeated itself, the Vix bumping the table and attacking it. Tate wondered how long, how many times this had repeated over and over again; months? Years?

Instead of pity, Tate felt loathing. He didn't see a person who once had loved and been loved, with hopes and family. He saw an inert thing, like the guts of a bomb, dormant, unremarkable, that is, until someone sparked the trigger unleashing terror, agony and death.

Rosse and Monkhouse watched, expectantly, as Tate lowered to a squat. The slowness of his movements mutely warned of danger and the need of silence.

With his eyes fixed on the window, Tate reached down to his belt and unsheathed his tomahawk. The all black tool had been with him though several tours of duty and countless ops. The handle was an incredibly tough kevlar, synthetic blend making it harder and more durable than hickory wood, yet lightweight with a sure grip. The head of the axe was high carbon steel with a classic curved blade. The other end of the head was a blunt spike, able to punch through sheet steel or body armor. Tate knew his tomahawk, its heft and balance like the back of his hand.

Grasping it by the head, he drew it out of the sheath then nodded readiness to Rosse and Monkhouse who nodded back, unsure what to expect. Using the handle, he tapped at the windowsill then flipped the tomahawk, catching the handle, the spike of the axe poised and ready.

An instant later a withered arm shot out of the darkened window, whipping blindly in the air, the naked, jagged bones of its fingers scrabbling open and closed.

To the others astonishment, Tate grabbed the arm and pulled. The Vix's head came into the light with a growl. The image was frozen in Monkhouse's mind. Long, black hair hung in dull, matted clumps from a leathery skull. The stretched skin pulled back the lips in a permanent snarl, exposing cracked teeth that snapped at Tate's hand.

Tate swung and buried the spike into its skull. The Vix went limp. With a yank, Tate freed his axe and shoved the thing back through the window.

"Ready for the main event?" said Tate, slipping the tomahawk back into its sheath. He pulled his rifle around and checked the safety then turned back towards the village.

"Why does it have to be an event?" whispered Monkhouse to Rosse.

The main road was just beyond their cluster of trees. Two wide gullies paralleled either side to slow down erosion from the frequent rains, but the storm and turned them into churning sluices.

Tate's attention was on the smoldering building across the road. The fire had left the front of the house a charred skeleton, the metal roof torn and bent from a powerful impact of the satellite. *That's where the satellite came down*, thought Tate. A low wall of stacked rocks created a courtyard around the front of the house with a sun faded, brown car inside. Tate tried to peer into the blackened mouth of the hole burned into the house, but from his distance it was impossible to make out anything. Even the storm wouldn't have been enough to deafen the noise of the satellite slamming into the house. If that hadn't attracted any Vix, there was a good chance the fire would.

"We cross the road single file," instructed Tate to Rosse and Monkhouse. "Heads on a swivel. Once on the other side you two take up position on the road side of that rock wall. I'm going to the car."

"Rock wall," said Rosse. "Got it."

"What happens next?" asked Monkhouse.

"Rosse, you'll give me overwatch, said Tate. "Anything hostile shows itself from that house, you put a grenade in its face. Monkhouse, you cover our six. Copy?"

"Copy," said both men.

Slowly, Tate leaned out of the brush and looked up and down the road. At best he could make out the dark forms of the further buildings, but nothing more. Rosse and Monkhouse stood and followed Tate as he stepped into the open. He jumped the first gully and fast walked across the road. With Rosse and Monkhouse following, Tate jumped the next gully then reached the low wall of the courtyard. Vaulting over that he sprinted the forty feet and hunkered down next to the car. Tate looked back and saw Rosse peering over the wall. They exchanged thumbs up then Tate turned his attention back to the blackened cavity of the house. The storm had turned the courtyard into a shallow pool of mud. Mud caked logs had washed away from a stack of firewood and littered the courtyard adding another obstacle Tate would have to maneuver around.

He badly wanted to see what might be in there. He could imagine digging around for the buried piece of satellite as Vix charged him, out of the darkness. There'd be no help from Rosse who wouldn't risk shooting blindly into the shadows.

Tate estimated it was another forty feet from his position to the house. Another building, ahead and to the right, sat just outside the low wall. Its single open window looking into the courtyard offered no cover for Tate to make his approach.

As he began to formulate his path of least exposure to the house, the wind suddenly gusted. Tate clapped a hand on his boonie hat before it could fly off and he looked down as one of the nearby muddy logs sluggishly tumbled against the tire of the car. Something about it was odd. It didn't fit what his mind was telling him he was looking at. He realized it was an arm.

His mind instantly ejected everything he thought he knew about his situation and a new realization slammed though his head.

Those weren't logs of firewood sunken in the mud. They were dead Vix. A lot of them, and somebody with serious firepower had wiped them all out. Tate's instincts redlined as he understood he had just walked into a kill zone and the moment he stepped out of cover he'd be another muddy corpse. He only needed this unknown threat to take their eyes off of him a second, or two; just long enough for Tate to reach the wall with Rosse and Monkhouse.

"Rosse!" yelled Tate. "Put a grenade in that house NOW!"

Rosse's head rose up as he aimed the grenade launcher when the stone wall, in front of him, was hammered with gunfire. Dust and sparks flew off the stone. Rosse flinched as he pulled the trigger and the grenade spiraled over the house, exploding somewhere in the trees.

Staying behind the cover of the car, Tate blind fired at the house, hoping to buy Rosse another shot at their attackers. Instantly, the car bucked as bullets thunked into the body of the car.

Monkhouse rolled onto his chest and looked at Rosse with wide eyes. "Holy crap," blurted Monkhouse as red tracers sizzled overhead. "What do we do?"

"Shoot back, ya moron!" yelled Rosse, hoping Monkhouse didn't hear the quiver in his voice.

Monkhouse peeked over the wall and glimpsed the front of the house. The inside of the house pulsed with light as gunfire lanced in his direction. He ducked down as the rock wall shuttered, bullets smacking into the stone, spraying hot splinters of lead and shards of rock.

Fear squeezed Monkhouse's heart, certain the instant he aimed over the wall his face would be turned to pulp. He laid his gun over the top of the wall, about to blind fire when Rosse kicked him in the side.

"You're gonna hit Top!"

"If I look out there they're gonna hit me!" screamed Monkhouse.

"Move an shoot," barked Rosse. "Don't shoot from the same place twice."

Rosse rolled away, popped up, and fired a burst into the house. Bullets peppered the rock wall just as Rosse ducked down. Grinning at Monkhouse, he gave a thumbs up and rolled to a new position.

Monkhouse rolled the other way causing the hood of his poncho to flap over his face. Cursing, he brushed it aside then with yell he sprang up and fired a burst at the house. The reaction was instantaneous as bullets ripped the air over his head, so close he could feel their heat.

He rolled to another position and fired again, taking cover and feeling a small confidence in his new tactic.

Tate slapped at his chest, feeling for the hard, plastic canister of his smoke grenade. Yanking it out of its sleeve he steadied his shaking finger from the adrenaline flooding his body and threaded it though the pull ring. He jerked out the ring and took his finger off the safety lever. The 'spoon' flew off with a sharp crack and white smoke instantly spouted from the top of the grenade. Risking a quick look at the house, Tate hurled the grenade. It bounced once on the front porch of the house and rolled in. With no time to spare, Tate braced himself against the car and shoved off towards the wall. Suddenly, geysers of mud erupted in front of him. Tate hurled himself back to the cover of the car as the unmistakable thump of a light machine-gun churned up the ground.

Rosse glanced over the wall long enough to see gouts of flame coming from the open window of the other building.

"Shoot the window!" yelled Rosse.

Monkhouse popped up from behind the wall and focused his fire on the window. To his horror the machine gun's blooms of fire swiveled towards him and he dove into the mud and rolled. The wall exploded as the machine gun cracked the rocks, knocking a hole where Monkhouse had just been.

Someone, inside the house, kicked Tate's smoke grenade back outside where it landed and sunk into the muddy ooze. White smoke bubbled up, but was swept away in the wind.

Tate saw the machine gun go to work, like a sledgehammer, on the rock wall Rosse and Monkhouse were using as cover. He knew they were pinned down and if either of them broke cover and ran they'd be cut in half.

Rosse fired a burst and his gun locked open. "Monkhouse, I'm empty," yelled Rosse, punching the wall with empty rage. But he got no response. An icy sickness clenched his gut as he saw Monkhouse, several feet away, curled up in a ball on the other side of the widening gap in the wall.

Ignoring the bullets tearing past him, Rosse dashed from cover and dove next to Monkhouse as bullets erupted spouts of mud close enough to splatter him. Unconcerned for his own safety, he began pulling at Monkhouse's poncho, looking for blood.

"I got ya buddy," said Rosse. "Take it easy. Tell me where ya got hit."

Monkhouse shuddered and looked up at Rosse with panicked eyes through his mud splattered face. "Where'd you come from?" muttered Monkhouse.

"Hey! Where're ya hit?" urged Rosse.

They both flinched as the machine gun rammed a stream of bullets next to them, pulverizing the wall in seconds.

"I'm not hit," said Monkhouse.

"What?" said Rosse, disbelieving. He jerked Monkhouse's gun from his hands and saw the magazine was nearly full.

"I can't do this," whimpered Monkhouse. "I thought I could, but I don't want to die."

Rosse's face flushed red and he punched Monkhouse in the face. Blood ran down his face, but Monkhouse hardly moved.

"That's Top out there," growled Rosse. "He'd give his life to save your ass any day and you're hide'n here while he's getting shot up?" Monkhouse grunted as Rosse shoved the gun back in his hands.

"You think I ain't scared, ya dickhead?" yelled Rosse. "I think I crapped myself, but you gotta fight because that's what we do for each other."

Monkhouse looked down at the gun in his hands then back at Rosse.

"I'm outta ammo," said Rosse. "If you don't fight we're all gonna die."

Monkhouse's eyes seemed to lose their glassy panic as he nodded through his shivering. He scrunched up onto his knees and brought his gun to his shoulder. "Nice knowing you," he said and then popped up from the wall.

His finger stopped before pressing the trigger as he saw several people standing near Tate who had his hands on his head. Monkhouse could see at least two of them had their guns pointed at Tate.

"Whoa, cowboy!" said Toby, from behind Monkhouse. There was an audible *click* as Toby cocked the hammer on his gun. "I think we're done with all that for today. Now, both of you put down your guns."

Rosse didn't need to be told twice and stood up, flinging his empty gun into the mud.

Tate's face was a mix of barely contained rage and frustration. He'd lead his people into a trap and had probably just cost them their lives. He would carry that regret to his grave, but he suspected that could be a short walk. Through the haze of rainfall, he saw someone with their gun to Monkhouse's head. Monkhouse dropped his gun then everything was black as someone blindfolded Tate.

———

Wesson, Fulton, Ota and Kaiden were hiking back to meet up with Tate and the only good news was the rain had finally stopped, but the jungle always had ways of punishing intruders. They began to stew in their ponchos and put them back in their packs, but the jungle was saturated and everything they touched dumped water on them. Soon they were soaked, their clothing clinging to their skin like a wet, sticky film, but the wetness brought no relief from the humidity.

The impact force of the downed satellite fragment had buried itself in the muddy ooze of dead, rotted plant material and animal dung. By the time they'd dug it out all of them were caked in the foul smelling muck only to discover this part of the satellite didn't contain the database.

No sooner had the rain stopped than the jungle came back to noisy life. Sounds echoed from the canopy high above and tree limbs rustled and snapped as monkeys screeched and chased each other in a fight for territory cheered on by the cries and howls of their clans.

The jungle stopped abruptly at the road which lead to the village. Everyone was grateful to be out of the soggy tangle of roots and vines and onto firmer ground. Wesson stopped the team, confirming everyone was present with a quick head-count before moving on.

"Anything from Tate?" Wesson asked Fulton.

"I haven't been able to reach him," said Fulton. "But this radio is junk. The weather seal is cracked all over the place." It was Fulton's pet complaint and he wasn't wrong. Patches of duct tape were all over the radio, plugging seams around the antenna sockets and covering splits in cable insulation.

The last word from Tate was a static filled transmission to join him at the village. As the first buildings of the village came into view, Wesson was keen for a situation report. They were tired and hungry, and she was looking forward to taking off her sodden boots and having something to eat.

Kaiden had been walking next to her since they'd reached the road. Taller than Kaiden, Wesson's view of her face was blocked by Kaiden's operator cap making it impossible to read her expression. If she had any concerns, she wasn't sharing them with Wesson. Kaiden moved with her typical easy pace, her gun cradled in her arms. Strands of auburn hair clung to the sides of her face, but most of it was kept out of the way in a tight braid.

"Kind of makes you forget what dry feels like," said Kaiden.

"Uh," mumbled Wesson. "Yeah."

Once again, Kaiden seemed to have sensed Wesson's thoughts, or had caught her sideways glance at her. The sensation that Kaiden could read her made Wesson uncomfortable.

Wesson preferred things out in the open. She always considered people who talked in subtext and innuendo were hiding something and that made them untrustworthy. Wesson was very conflicted about Kaiden. She ticked all of Wesson's boxes on her list of things to be suspicious of, but on the other hand Kaiden had saved her life. It made it hard for Wesson to know how to classify her; which was another thing that bothered her about Kaiden.

"Do you smell that?" asked Kaiden.

Wesson took a moment to refocus on the here and now then recognized the smell. Looking up she saw a tendril of smoke rising above the trees. She wasn't alarmed, but it made sense to approach with caution.

The road bent around the high trees and opened to the village. Water dripped off metal clad roofs as they made their way deeper into the village until they stopped in front of a string of homes lining the left side of the road; across from them was a home set further back with a courtyard bordered by a crumbling, low rock wall. The smell of smoke was stronger and they could see the charred damage to the front of the home.

Ota was the first to see the bullet holes. "We should move," he said, crouching.

Wesson turned to see what Ota was talking about. The front of the building was peppered with bullet holes and by the look of the exposed wood, they were fresh.

"Everyone spread out," said Wesson, "and..."

Her next words froze in her throat as several gun barrels sprang from the building's windows.

"Take it easy," warned a voice from the shadows of the building they were facing.

Reflex made the team begin to crouch, preparing to fire, but all of them understood that would be suicide.

"Drop the guns," said the voice in a curiously friendly way.

Wesson didn't know why, but was surprised that Kaiden was the first to surrender her weapon. Fulton followed her example and then Ota. Wesson was the last as she slowly eased the light machine gun to the ground.

"You guys are doing great," said the voice. "Now, turn around and put your hands behind your backs. Some of my friends are going to tie your wrists. I know somebody's thinking that'll be the best time to fight back, or take a hostage. I know that's what I'd be thinking, but just between us, that thinking will get all of you killed."

Wesson and the others turned around putting their hands behind their backs. There was the sound of footsteps in the mud then suddenly something ridged slipped around their wrists and was cinched tight.

There was nothing Kaiden could do now, except collect as much information about their captures as she could. She quickly looked over at the man tying up Wesson. There were no wasted movements, no smiles of victory. The soldiers eyes remained watchful for any attempts to fight back. Then a blindfold covered Kaiden's eyes and she bent her mind to focus on her other sense. She felt hands roughly pat her down for other weapons. The hands didn't linger or molest her. This was a professional soldier who's focus on a single objective.

Each of the captives were held by the shoulder strap of their tactical vests and lead to another part of the village. The soldiers never said a word, but someone in their group was humming.

It might have been a small thing, but it made Kaiden change her mind about getting out of this alive.

She reasoned he captors had plenty of opportunities to kill them. They could have easily ambushed them on the road. Wesson, Fulton, Ota and herself would all be dead mowed down in an instant. When the guns appeared from the windows they weren't shot, but told to disarm. Even now, bound, blind and helpless they could be executed with no trouble. Instead these soldiers wanted to take them out of action, but the humming.

That person was a wildcard. Not like the other soldiers, this one felt like he picked and chose which rules he'd follow as his mood suited him. That made him unpredictable and dangerous.

Kaiden was shaken from her thoughts as someone firmly pushed her against a wall, the meaning was clear. *Stay!*

Her head was tugged forward as the blindfold was untied and removed. Squinting in anticipation of the bright light, her eyes quickly adjusted to her new surroundings. Before her were six, armed men in jungle camo and tactical gear. To her left was Fulton and

Wesson, also bound, but blindfolds removed. To her right was Ota and, to her relief, Tate, Rosse and Monkhouse.

"Lets dump these losers and go," said Andy.

"I'm setting some ground rules first," said one of the other men.

"Rules?" said Andy. "C'mon Hall. Who plays by rules?"

"All right, listen up," said Hall, ignoring Andy, as he stepped up to his prisoners. "It doesn't take a rocket scientist to know you're here for the satellite, same as us." Looking up and down at the bound team members he sighed as he scratched his chin though his reddish, brown beard. "Our job is to get the satellite. Nobody's been hurt, and I'm good with it staying that way. We're leaving you here, tied up. We checked the area and you don't have to worry about Vix, at least for a while. By then you'll be out of those cuffs." He nodded to the pile of captured weapons he stood next to. "We're leaving your weapons so you can get back to your helo in once piece." He swatted at something on his neck, cursing under his breath. "Now you're thinking if you move fast enough you'll catch up to us and take the satellite, but you're not going to do that because that man," he said, pointing to Fernandez, holding his sniper rifle, "will rag-doll your ass before you ever hear the shot."

11

CHOICES

"We see anybody within a klick of us and we'll take all of you out," said Hall, pointing at them. "Go home."

Hall turned back to his team, but stopped as Tate spoke up for the first time.

"Do you know how dangerous the information is, inside that satellite?" growled Tate.

"Knowing isn't part of the job," said Hall.

"The people who hired you will use that to throw an entire country into chaos," said Tate.

Hall paused, studying Tate as he considered what he'd heard. He inhaled, about to say something.

"The country?" interrupted Andy, walking up, next to the bearded merc.

"I got this," stated Hall.

"This guy's a true believer," continued Andy unabated. "You all look like raggedy militia, but you aren't, are you."

Except for the Grave Diggers unit patch on their shoulders, nobody in Tate's team wore any form of identification or rank. Andy walked up and yanked the velcro patch off Tate's shoulder.

"We don't have time for this," pushed Hall. "We have a short window to get back to camp and up-link the intel."

The patch had been Tate's idea and his rookie team had eagerly adopted it. A red bordered shield with a field of green. On it was a black dagger through a scowling, white skull. Across the grip of the dagger was a red banner with the unit's motto, "Remorseless Relentless".

About to toss it on the ground, Andy gave it a second look. "Now that's some balls," said Andy. "That's a Fairbairn Sykes dagger." Andy held up the patch for his team to see, but they were uninterested. "You guys know who has that same dagger in their patch?" he asked.

"That's those US Army Special Ops Command, dudes," said Fernandez.

"That's Delta Force," said Hall.

"Give that man a gold star," said Andy. Tate glowered at him as Andy slapped the patch back on his shoulder with a grin.

He looked down and saw Tate's empty leather holster. All of their gear was dated, but Tate's holster was a real antique. His great-grandfather wore it in World War Two. Tate had found it rummaging through the attic, as a small boy, and wore it every chance he could. He still remembered how his small, toy cap pistol rattled around inside of it and the first day it held his Colt 1911. Although battered and scuffed, even today, the large "US" embossed on the flap of the M1912 holster was easily visible.

Andy looked closely at Tate's face, intrigued by something until recognition lit his eyes and a boyish smile spread across his face. "No. It can't be."

He quickly went to the pile of weapons and pushed off the top guns with the toe of his boot.

There was a collective groan of protest from the other mercenaries.

"What're you doing?" called Fernandez unhappily. "What's he doing, man?"

Hall shook his head in exasperation and leaned into Andy's ear. "You have been a pain in everyone's ass from the moment we put boots on the ground. I'm getting paid to run this op and bring back that satellite, and I'm telling you to get back with the others, or I'll leave you here."

In answer Andy picked up Tate's tomahawk and 1911 pistol and showed them to Hall as he went back to Tate.

"Tiller?" said Andy. "Is that you?"

"You know him?" asked Hall.

Turning to the other mercenaries, Andy held up the weapons. "Guys, I want you to meet my old Delta Force team leader." He turned back to face Tate with a big smile. "Sergeant, First Class, Jack Tiller of the 471st Special Missions Unit. The Night Devils."

"I remember you," growled Tate.

"Tiller?" puzzled Fulton quietly to Monkhouse.

"Shut up," hissed Monkhouse, but Andy had heard him and walked over to Fulton.

"I ran Delta ops with a guy that carried this tomahawk and beat up, piece of junk," said Andy, holding the Colt .45. "His name was Tiller." Andy tapped the flat side of the tomahawk on Fulton chest. "What do you call him?"

Fulton flattened himself against the wall, away from the sharp blade that glistened inches from his throat. Swallowing hard he said nothing else and did his best to look straight ahead, ignoring Andy.

Andy walked up to each team member, looking at their patch then scrutinizing each of them with a smile. "You aren't Delta," he said to Wesson. "Nope, not you, or you," he said as he studied each of them, and stopped in front of Kaiden.

Unlike the others, who either glared at him, or ignored him, she smiled back, unfazed, keeping eye contact with Andy. Putting his hand on the wall just above Kaiden's shoulder, Andy leaned in close to her. "One of these things is not like the others."

"I was just thinking the same about you," said Kaiden.

"Damn, Kaiden. It's good to see you again. When was the last time we were together? El Salvador? Syria?"

"Fort Bragg," smiled Kaiden. "Your court martial."

"By the way, thanks for that."

"I'm a fixer," said Kaiden. "It's what I do." She leaned around Andy to look at the other mercenaries, their patience running out. "You don't exactly fit in with your new friends, but fitting in never interested you."

"Thanks for the compliment." He leaned in close to her ear and whispered, "Just between you and me, I don't think they like me." Andy saw Tate scowling at him and chuckled. "I *know* he doesn't like me."

"Imagine that," said Kaiden, unruffled.

"I bet you don't like me either," said Andy, opening the space between them.

"Cut me loose," said Kaiden with an icy smile, "and lets find out."

Andy laughed and stepped back. "I have a feeling that would be the last mistake I ever made." He pulled up his shirt exposing his lean, but muscled chest and waist, disfigured by a mangled scar that scrawled across his left side. "I got this from making the mistake of trusting that guy," he said pointing the pistol at Tate. Then he waved the gun up and down the line of prisoners. "Now you got a new bunch of clueless bullet-catchers following you around like baby ducks. Do they know the mistake they're making?"

Andy raised his voice so the tied captives could hear him. "When I got opened up from a frag, that he LEFT ME!" Andy shouted, flaring with anger, "The mission comes first. Right Jack?" Andy's flash of anger vanished with disturbing suddenness. He laughed at a joke only he could hear.

Tate's lips pressed together until they turned white. His eyes couldn't hide the smoldering anger building inside him. "That's not what happened, growled Tate.

"Loyalty? Honor? No man left behind?" queried Andy. "I thought it was me. I wasn't worthy of the revered Jack Tiller."

Tate glared in silence, his hands balled into fists, turning purple as they strained against the thick nylon cuffs.

"But it's not just me. Nobody comes before the mission." Andy stepped up to Tate, nearly nose to nose. "Even when it means leaving his little girl to die."

Tate's face twisted with rage. With a guttural yell he drove forward slamming his head into Andy's face. Bone crunched and Andy staggered back, dropping Tate's pistol and tomahawk, as his eyes rolled up into his head. Blood streamed from his broken nose, and bubbled from his lips.

Everyone stood frozen in astonishment. A couple of mercenaries started towards Tate, but Hall blocked them with his arm. Taking the hint they settled back. Arms resting on his assault rifle, Hall watched the dazed Andy with a hint of amusement.

Tate crashed backwards into the wall, the bands around his wrists snapping under the force, and charged Andy.

Shaking away the star bursts from his vision, Andy had no time to react as Tate hammered his fist into Andy's gut. Blood and spit sprayed from Andy as he doubled over and sat heavily on the soggy ground.

Tate moved in, but was checked with a warning from Hall. "Let the man get up," he ordered.

"Hot damn," wheezed Andy, as he rocked from side to side, trying to breath with aching lungs. "Did I hit a nerve?" He touched his face and grinned as his hand came away covered in blood. Andy sat up, propping himself up with his hands and looked up at the raging Tate.

"Get up!" commanded Tate. In spite of Hall's casual demeanor, Tate knew the man would shoot him if he tried to attack Andy while he was on the ground, but the anger pumping through him said it would be worth it.

Andy raised his hands as a show of compliance and lifted himself out of the mud. "I get it," panted Andy. "You don't want these idiots knowing what you are."

Tate fired a staggering right cross at Andy's jaw, but he was ready this time and easily deflected the blow.

"That you'll bail on them the moment things go bad," said Andy, as he side stepped and thew a solid punch into Tate's ribs. With a groan, Tate turned and tried to grab Andy's arm who slipped out of the grab and landed another punch.

Tate bellowed and came at Andy with a rage his team had never seen before. He swung a balled fists in a whirl of raw emotion, but Andy easily, playfully slipped past the flesh and bone sledgehammers flying at him.

"You got old, Jack," said Andy landing a painful kick to Tate's thigh.

His leg collapsed and Tate fell to the mud like a toppled tree. Andy lightly bobbed back and forth, holding his hands in loose fists.

With a burst of energy, Tate came off the chewed up, muddy ground, flailing bone-shattering blows; each one deflected. Tate grunted as Andy him punished with every miss, landing blow after blow until Tate's face was a battered mess of blood and meat. His breath came in ragged jags as Tate shambled to face Andy, but his left eye was swollen shut and his right blurred with smeared blood, making it impossible to find his target.

"That's it," said Hall, having seen enough. "You're done."

Tate sunk to his knees then collapsed, face first, into the mud.

Andy's blood smeared face was a grotesque mask of amusement. "Woooooo! That felt good," he cheered, bouncing on his feet. "I mean, I must've imagined the sweet beat down I'd give you a hundred times, but this, this was better."

Hall walked over and rolled Tate onto his back, choking on mud as he gasped for air. "You should have let him bleed out on that op," he said quietly to Tate. "Would have saved me from having to put up with him now."

"I didn't leave him," muttered Tate.

Andy put his hands on his knees, catching his breath, and looked at the angry faces of Tate's team. "You think I'm the bad guy." Straightening up, Andy shuffled over and picked up the dropped tomahawk and Colt .45. "You believe he wouldn't abandon any of you for this mission?"

Suddenly the wide, gapping barrel of Tate's pistol was pointed at the team. Ear ringing thunder clapped as the big Colt shot out a ball of fire. The sound snapped Tate's foggy head back into focus and he was on his feet without knowing he'd done it. Hall was running towards the gunfire yelling something amid shouts of fear and anger. A lone scream cut through the chaos.

Hall collided with Andy, ripping the gun from his hand as Tate ran past him to his huddled team. The wall behind them was splattered with blood. Part of Tate wanted to stop, simply wink out of existence before this nightmare went on.

Rosse was knelt over, snarling curses, demanding to be cut loose, calling for his medkit. Everything was a confusion of voices and people, blocking Tate's view of the body laying on the ground. He grabbed someone's shoulder, he didn't know who, and flung them aside. Blood laid on the muddy ground reflecting sunlight with a surrealistic iridescence.

Pushing his way through, Tate's heart stopped as he looked down into Kaiden's agonized face. His eyes traveled over her, looking for a wound among splatters of mud.

A meaty hand wrapped around Tate's wrist and yanked him to his knees. Looking up, Rosses face, inches from Tate's, was yelling something.

"Press here!" barked Rosse. "Hard."

He pushed Tate's hand down on Kaiden's thigh, who lurched up, screaming, clutching at Tate's hand. Blood seeped between Tate's dirty fingers, and realizing what Rosse wanted him to do he moved his palm over the wound and pressed down.

Tate didn't see how Rosse got his medical bag, it just appeared in his hands.

"Get a tourniquet," yelled Tate.

"Move your hand," ordered Rosse, ignoring him.

Tate took away his hand and Rosse washed the area with a bottle of water. For the first time Tate could clearly see the wound. Kaiden's pants had been cut open revealing her thigh. He saw a dark, red hole as wide as his thumb, but it disappeared as blood welled up and spilled out.

Rosse ripped open a foil packet and emptied white powder on the wound. "Hang on," said Rosse. "You're gonna feel a lot better in just a sec." He took out a fat syringe from his bag and pulled off the outer covering then pushed it deep into the wound.

Kaiden cried in agony as hands held her down. Thick, white foam, tinged with pink, fizzed up around the wound as Rosse slowly pulled the syringe out of her leg. Seconds later, Kaiden stoped squirming and her face relaxed as the pain subsided and her breathing slowed to normal.

"I gave her a wound-packing hemostat," explained Rosse. "It's got a localized painkiller that'll last for a while."

"How bad is it?" asked Tate, his face lined with worry.

"We get her on the Moth and to a real hospital," said Rosse, "she keeps the leg, but that hemostat's temporary and we gotta get moving right now. Otherwise, between the blood loss and shock..." Rosse ended there, but his expression told Tate the horrible outcome.

Fury boiled through Tate, driving him to his feet and looking for the target of his vengeance.

Hall had been standing behind him, and wasn't about to move out of the way. "I know what you're thinking, brother, but that's not going to happen."

Further away, two of the mercs had Andy by the arms, roughly walking him to the edge of the jungle.

"Now you'll see!" shouted Andy. "He'll let her die. Mission first, right Tiller?"

Tate briefly looked at the pile of weapons only a few feet away, then back at Andy. Hall followed his glance and stepped up close to Tate.

"Nothing's changed," said Hall. "We go our way and you go home."

Tate gave no sign he'd heard Hall, but kept his eyes locked on Andy.

"Hey," snapped Hall, moving his face in front of Tate's. "Are you receiving me? Coming after us is only going to get you and all your people dead. You copy?"

Tate's focus broke and he looked deflated as his anger left him. "Yeah, I, uh, copy," he said, meeting Hall's eyes.

Hall considered Tate for a moment then nodded in approval. "Safe trails," he said, backing a few steps before turning away and heading after his people.

Tate turned around as several of his team were gently lifting Kaiden out of the mud.

After a quick search of the surrounding homes they found a narrow, wooden bed frame to use as a stretcher.

· · ·

Carrying Kaiden, the team marched on in silence, heading back to camp. Tate walked behind them, his face a granite mask of hate. The team traded looks, asking unspoken questions about Andy and how much of what he said was true.

Without a word Tate stopped, his eyes fixed on the ground before him.

The rest of the team walked on until Wesson saw Tate just standing there. She called everyone back as Tate took out a map and studied it.

"Uh, Top?" ventured Rosse. "We have ta get Kaiden to a hospital, okay?"

"What's he doing?" whispered Fulton.

Tate looked between the map and the way they'd come.

"Sergeant Major," said Wesson, tactfully, "I'd sure like to know what you're doing."

"Yer kidding me, right?" said Rosse under his breath. "He's think'n of going back."

"Huh?", said Fulton. "Back? But Kaiden..."

"Quiet down," ordered Wesson. "Top? We have to get Kaiden to a hospital."

"Radio!" called Tate.

Fulton, who carried the teams field radio, also carried a corner of Kaiden's stretcher. Rattled, he didn't know if he should let go, or pull everyone with him, until Ota walked over and offered to take his place with the stretcher. Grateful, Fulton nodded thanks then trotted to Tate's side.

Tate pulled the handset from the radio pouch on Fulton's back and dialed in a frequency.

Rosse, Wesson, Ota and Monkhouse put the stretcher down, under the shade of a cluster of tall trees. Rosse started to march over to Tate, but Wesson stopped him.

"He's doing it," groused Rosse. "It's just like that guy said."

"Shut up," barked Wesson. "We don't know what he's doing."

There was a click over the radio and Nathan's voice came through. "Tate?"

"Yeah," grunted Tate.

"Something's wrong," said Nathan.

"There was another team after Vulcan 4. They got it and Kaiden's been shot."

"How did they get it?" asked Nathan.

Tate looked over at Monkhouse, who turned away, feeling miserable. Kaiden's ashen face was looking up at him and Monkhouse felt a sharp pang of guilt.

"I'm so sorry,' he said.

She looked puzzled, then a lopsided smile curled the corners of her mouth causing Monkhouse to wonder if she heard him, or if the painkiller was messing with her head.

Monkhouse's attention was drawn by Tate's brittle voice as he explained they'd just blown the mission.

"We were ambushed," admitted Tate.

"Return the favor and get Vulcan 4 back," said Nathan.

"I have a casualty that requires a hospital."

"I hate to be the voice of reason, but you're worried about one person," said Nathan, "at the risk of thousands."

Tate gripped the radio wishing he could strangle it. "I'll get back to you." He disconnect the transmission without waiting for a reply and stood with his fists on his hips unmindful of the heat and humidity. He angrily slapped hard at something buzzing his ear and missed making his ear ring with pain. He could feel the pressure of anger and frustration straining his self control.

Tate headed for Kaiden, leaving Fulton wondering if he should stay or follow. Everyone found someplace else to be, giving Tate extra space, except Rosse who hardly moved, staring accusingly at Tate.

Kneeling down next to Kaiden, Tate forced himself to look away from the red stained bandage, knowing underneath it was a mangled hole from his own gun. He pushed the thought out of his mind and forced himself to smile at her. "What have I told you about picking up on strange men?"

Kaiden gave an uneven smile and chuckled. "What's the plan?"

"We need to get you to a hospital," said Tate.

"You know what I mean."

Tate's smile disappeared and he looked over his shoulder, from where they'd come. "That is the plan."

"Damn right," mumbled Rosse, who was near enough to eavesdrop while pretending to look at the distant hills.

Kaiden's eyes wandered for a moment before coming back to Tate. She looked at him, confused, as if she didn't remember he was there, then her expression lost its softness as her thoughts refocused. "Why are you here?"

Tate shrugged and looked away with a pained expression as he battled with conflicting demons. Each choice was both right and wrong. He felt a tug on his shoulder as Kaiden peeled the unit patch from his sleeve.

Surprised, he looked wondering at her until she faced the patch towards him and tapped her finger under the embroidered words of their motto. *Remorseless, Relentless.*

It only took an instant for understanding to ignite in Tate's mind. The tangle of conflicts, demanding his allegiance, were silenced and the weight bearing down on his shoulders slipped away.

He grinned down at her as she offered back his patch. Standing up, he put the patch back on his shoulder and looked around at the expectant faces of his team.

"Monkhouse. Rosse," said Tate firmly. "Get your gear. Top off your rations from the rest of the team."

"Whoa, what's go'n on?" asked Rosse.

"We're getting the database," said Tate as he pulled out two pouches of rations from Fulton's pack. "That's why we're here. Wesson? You, Ota, and Fulton are going back to the Moth and fly Kaiden to the nearest base hospital."

"Yes, *Sergeant Major*," said Wesson, pointedly dropping a warning for Rosse to dial it down.

But Rosse wasn't taking the hint.

"What about my patient?" said Rosse. "Am I just supposed to leave her?"

"Did you stop the bleeding?" asked Tate, not looking up from checking the supplies in his pack.

"Yeah," said Rosse.

"Did you screw up her bandage?"

"No," growled Rosse. "I didn't *screw* up anything."

"Then she doesn't need a medic," said Tate. He picked up Rosse's pack and tossed it to him. "I do."

"So it's like what that guy said," said Rosse. "You're gonna chose the mission over your own..."

"ROSSE!" barked Wesson. She got up in the stocky man's face, glaring, unblinkingly, in his eyes. "You were given an order. If you have anything else to say besides 'Yes sergeant major' you can say it to me."

The muscles in Rosse's jaw flexed like he was grinding stone as he stared back. There was nothing in Wesson that said she cared that he was bigger, stronger and had fifty pounds on her and Rosse knew it.

"Yes... sergeant major," muttered Rosse.

Wesson nodded and left. Without a word, Rosse retrieved his pack and busied himself with checking his supplies.

"Fulton," called Tate, as he returned to his pack.

Fulton jogged over to him and Tate took out the handset. A moment later Nathan picked up.

"Change of plans?" asked Nathan.

"Change of plans," said Tate. "We're going after the satellite, but we might have another problem. I overheard one of the mercs say they were going to uplink Vulcan 4 when they returned to their camp, and transmit everything in the database. By now they're outside the range of our tracker, which all but guarantees we'll be too late to stop them. The short version is we're screwed."

12

CHANGE OF PLANS

"You have more time than you think," said Nathan.

"That's what I was thinking," said Tate, sharply. "Otherwise you'd get to the point instead of dragging this out."

"I'm guessing you don't get asked to a lot of parties," joked Nathan.

"Do you?"

"Fair enough," conceded Nathan, after a moment's pause. "So, about that uplink. Vulcan 4 uses a P.E.E.F. A proprietary encrypted, eccentric frequency and it won't talk to anything that's not using the same frequency."

"What's to keep them from modifying a receiver to intercept the signal?"

"Nothing," said Nathan. "They've probably already done it."

"Where's the part about having more time than I think?" pressed Tate.

"That's the eccentric part," said Nathan. "Vulcan 4 continuously alternates the frequency. Their receiver knows to look for that signal, but it has to decipher the signal pattern and that takes a long time. Only after that happens can they send the data."

"I'm impressed. I didn't think The Ring was that technically advanced."

"I don't want to blow my own horn," said Nathan, "but they weren't until they hired me."

"You set up that receiver?" asked Tate in disbelief. "Who's side are you on?"

"A more sensitive person would be hurt by that question," said Nathan. "I didn't say the receiver works."

"It doesn't work?"

"No, it works like a charm," said Nathan. "Just not the way The Ring wanted. When they activate Vulcan 4 the receiver will appear to go though the motions of deciphering the frequency, but I built in my own functionality."

"Including geo-tracking?" prompted Tate.

"Bullseye. They'll be expecting the hand-shake between Vulcan 4 and the receiver to take a few hours. That should buy you the time you need to catch up to them."

Tate checked the satellite tracker and saw the location of Vulcan 4 had changed.

"I just sent you...," began Nathan.

"I see it," said Tate. "Anything else?"

"No."

"You can reach me on my sat-phone. Out," said Tate and disconnected the line.

Tate slung his pack over his shoulders and walked over to Wesson, who was talking to Kaiden.

"I'm Oscar, Mike," said Tate. "Are you good to go?"

"Yes," said Wesson.

He knelt down next to Kaiden, maintaining a business as usual attitude. "I'll see you in a couple days," said Tate.

Kaiden studied his battered face before meeting his eyes. "Stay away from Andy," she mumbled. "He'll kill you."

Tate craved the chance to catch up to Andy, but wasn't going to argue with her about it. "See you soon," he said, patting her on the shoulder.

Stifling a groan, he pushed himself back to his feet and addressed Wesson. "After you get her taken care of, come back and wait for us here."

Monkhouse and Rosse walked up, giving Tate a nod that they were ready.

"Don't worry about Kaiden," said Wesson. "I have this."

"I know, sergeant," smiled Tate. "That's why you're my second in command. If things go according to plan, we'll be back here in 48 hours."

"Copy that, Top," replied Wesson. Tate glanced at the tracker, checking the position of Vulcan 4, then motioned to Monkhouse and Rosse to follow him.

With the first few steps, the conflict and doubt Tate had been battling melted away. *This was the right move*, he thought, and felt his energy lift, fed by renewed purpose.

"Hey Top?" said Monkhouse.

"Right here," said Tate.

"Didn't the three of us go up against these guys just a few hours ago?"

"Yes, we did."

"If I remember right, that didn't work out so well."

Tate touched one of the cuts on his face, feeling the crusted blood mingled with his eyebrow. "No," said Tate. "It did not."

"And now we're doing the same thing again?"

"That's right."

"Why?" puzzled Monkhouse.

"The first time they were ready for us," said Tate, "and we weren't. This time it's the other way around."

"Something's wrong," said Andy as he stood by the fire watching the flickering glow on the surrounding jungle. "It's taking too long."

Vulcan 4 sat next to a signal booster and four small, black boxes with fibre optic cables attaching them in a daisy chain.

Hall read the status display which showed the power levels were strong and Vulcan 4 was transmitting. Telemetry from the receiver confirmed they were making a connection, but the receiver still hadn't deciphered the signal pattern.

"They said it could take a long time for the receiver to sync up," said Hall.

"How long?" persisted Andy.

A mercenary stepped out of the darkened jungle and slung his rife over his shoulder. "It's your watch, psycho."

"It's Andy," he grinned. "Why're you guys wired so tight? Your soldier days are over."

The merc stared at Andy, his face void of expression. "It's your watch," he said then slipped inside one of the single-man tents, that ringed the clearing between the campfire and the border of dense foliage.

"I'm racking out too," said Hall as he stood, brushing dirt from his knees.

"What about the satellite?" asked Andy.

"It can run overnight. If it hasn't uploaded by morning then I'll call our mission lead for instructions. Either way, don't sweat it. They're paying four times my contract fee, so whatever's in that satellite is valuable enough that they'll make sure it gets uploaded."

Andy picked up his assault rifle, checking there was a round in the chamber and the magazine was full. "You're ex-Army Rangers, right?"

"You have something to say about Rangers?" asked Hall.

"Not me," said Andy, with as much casual provocation as anyone could put into two words. "You know, kind of explains why you're only getting four times the going rate."

"And what? Because you're ex-Delta they're paying you more?"

"Hey, I never said they were paying me more than you," chuckled Andy, "just because I'm Delta."

"Delta couldn't hold the bucket a Ranger's pisses in," fumed Hall.

"I'm not saying Delta's better than Rangers," said Andy. "I mean, yeah, Delta beat Rangers three times running in the Best Ranger Competition and that's got to hurt. Losing at your own challenge."

"You've been rubbing everyone raw from day one of this op," said Hall. "I thought it was because you're a class-A prick, but that's not it. You're pushing buttons hoping one of us takes a swing at you. That would violate their contract. Less men means the op is harder and the Adversity and Hinderance bonus pay scale kicks in."

"That's a very clever plan, but you're giving me a lot more credit than I deserve. I'm just a guy doing a job. Maybe I get on some peoples nerves," shrugged Andy, "but it's not my fault Rangers get paid less than Delta."

"How have you lived this long without someone fragging you?" asked Hall.

Andy chuckled, hiding the movement of his thumb switching the safety of his gun from "SAFE" to "FIRE". "Kind of an overreaction for a little, friendly joking." Andy sighed and the smile ebbed away from his face. "But the ones that tried only made that mistake once."

The two men stared at each other for a long time, their faces giving no hint of their next move. The snap of the fire sounded unreasonably loud, but the world around them seemed to edge away, distancing itself from the brewing violence threatening to explode.

Halls shoulders relaxed, and just like that, the static charge dissipated.

"That's not the way I work," said Hall. "I kill out of self defense. Less demons to carry on my back."

"Huh, that's funny," said Andy.

"What's funny about it?"

"My demons are the ones still living."

Hall unzipped the front of his tent, taking off his boots before going inside. "It's your watch."

The jungle was a different place at night. The mingled cacophony of animal calls died away as the sun went down, knowing there was safety in silence. Night was the realm of predators and one of them was stalking the sleeping mercenaries.

Tate crept through the blackness, his movements deliberate, easing into every handhold and footstep, transferring his weight without a sound betraying him. The flicker of the mercs campfire was close enough to hear it.

At the moment all of his focus was on a thin, nylon filament strung tautly across his path.

"Monkhouse," whispered Tate into his radio. "I have a job for you."

Monkhouse silently apologized as he squeezed by an indignant Rosse who hadn't wavered from his sullen anger at Tate's decision to put the mission above his team.

Squinting in the blackness, Monkhouse moved slowly, able only to make out shapes once he was in arms reach. He felt he'd been seeking Tate forever when his fingers brushed his back.

"Found another one," said Tate. "Do your thing."

Monkhouse took 'pin-light' flashlight from his pocket and shined the minute beam on the boobytrap.

As the teams engineer, Monkhouse drew on his eclectic experience to maintain equipment in the field, build temporary structures, and in this case defuse boobytraps. How he knew about so many things was a mystery to Tate. Monkhouse hadn't shared his past, but Tate suspected it was a colorful one.

After a few seconds Monkhouse turned off the flashlight and quietly turned back to Tate. "It's not armed," he whispered.

"Say again?" said Tate.

"The trip wire's just for show," said Monkhouse. "Look."

Before Tate could stop him, Monkhouse tugged the nylon thread. Tate expected an explosion, but nothing happened. That didn't do anything for the adrenaline suddenly pumping through his body.

"See?" grinned Monkhouse.

Tate swallowed his heart and held his fist up in front of Monkhouse.

"Don't ever do that again," said Tate.

They'd gone another twenty feet when Tate found another boobytrap. The mercenaries had set up several of these around their camp as an early warning system.

His suspicions began to tingle when Monkhouse reported that, like the last trap, this one was dormant. It didn't make sense. *Why weren't the traps armed? Why wasn't anyone on watch?*

Tate had carefully reconned the entire camp, and couldn't believe there was no guard, roving or concealed. *I gave these mercs a lot more credit*, thought Tate. Gaps in the foliage allowed him narrow glimpses into the camp where he saw no sign of security there, either. Yet he knew men were in the tents from the occasional snores.

He could have sat there all night guessing and second guessing if was a trap, or they were being watched even now, or if the mercs were really that sloppy. No matter the answer, he had a mission to complete.

Tate crept back to where he'd left Rosse and Monkhouse and laid out his plan, drawing a crude diagram of the camp in the dirt. "Think of the camp like a clock face. We'll enter the camp from three different directions. Two, six and ten o'clock."

"Is it a good idea to split up?" asked Monkhouse. The guilt of freezing in combat, getting his team captured and Kaiden being shot was fresh in his mind, and here he was again, being depended on in a coming firefight. Anxiety and doubts began to churn in his stomach. He inhaled, about to blurt out he couldn't do this.

"Something on your mind?" asked Tate.

"No," said Monkhouse. He couldn't bring himself to say the words. If he had any doubts these men considered him a coward, he'd only confirm it by confessing his fears. "I was thinking strength in numbers. That's all."

"Our strength is that we'll have them in a crossfire," said Tate. "I'll take the ten position. Rosse, you're at two and Monkhouse is six."

"Great," said Monkhouse. "Uh, where's six?"

Of the three of them, Tate knew Monkhouse was the least skilled in stealth and chose the 'six' position because it was the shortest distance from their current position.

"That cluster of trees," said Tate pointing to a stand of trees forty feet behind them. "Once all of us are in position we go in cool and quiet."

"Slow is smooth," said Rosse.

"And smooth is fast," finished Monkhouse.

With a grin, Tate nodded and the men split up.

Position 'six' was thirty meters away, a short distance for

Monkhouse to cover, but Tate had hammered into him the mortality of making noise.

He hoped to steady his mind by concentrating on each small detail of his noise discipline training. *Breathe through the nose. Keep knees bent. Don't lock the hips. Something, something path. Something heel something toe.*

Monkhouse cursed himself for not having paid closer attention, or maybe he did but couldn't remember. The memory of cowering behind that low, rock wall as gunfire ripped into the car Tate used for cover was raw in his mind. The sound of Tate's voice screaming for help. The look of disbelief and shame on Rosse's face. He'd failed the men he called friend. Neither of them had mentioned it since then, but Monkhouse's guilt drove him to wonder if there wasn't a subtext of reproach behind everything they did and said.

He battled with himself, refusing to believe fear was stronger than his loyalty, and at the same time condemning himself because he was afraid.

Here was his chance to prove to them, and himself, he wouldn't give in to fear and he was failing miserably.

With a massive effort of will he forced himself to take a quiet, cleansing breath, and settle his mind. The fear was still there, but muted enough Monkhouse could think clearly. *Move.* He made that his only thought and once he took his first step the grip of fear began to loosen.

Ten meters closer to his position, Monkhouse was sweating with the effort of moving quietly. Every step demanded he gently test the ground under his boot, adding small amounts of pressure, feeling for the spring of twigs, the roll of loose rock, etc. If safe he'd slowly transfer his weight from one leg to the other. Making sure he felt stable and could keep his balance as he repeated the movement, over and over.

It's like torture version of Tai Chi, he thought and nearly let a nervous snicker escape.

Tensed and legs burning, Monkhouse reached his destination. Through the screen of tall ferns he could see the circle of tents ringing the low flicker of the dying campfire, but there was no one visible. That didn't mean the enemy wasn't watching. He thought about Tate and Rosse, how far they got in reaching their positions and how soon they'd check in. *Would the sound of the radio leak?* Monkhouse reached up, very slowly so as to not attract attention, and pressed his radio's earbud snugly into his ear then lowered his hand with the same care. There was nothing else to do but wait.

As the minutes ticked by Monkhouse's tension gave way to boredom, then fatigue. He fought against his drooping eyes, or thought he was until he his chin fell forward. His eyes popped open and his head snapped back up, but nothing had changed. The jungle around him hummed, and chirped in a droning lullaby, softly drifting him to sleep.

What was that? Monkhouse's head snapped up, his eyes went wide in alarm. *There was a sound. Did I dream it?* He listened, waiting for the sound to happen again. His brow furrowed in concentration. *What did I hear? I don't hear anything now.* Seconds ticked by as he waited for a sound, sure he'd heard something, but maybe not. *I don't hear anything now.* The suspicion persisted he hadn't dreamed it. *What am I missing?*

A new expression crawled across Monkhouse's face leaving his eyes's wide and his jaw slack. What was missing was sound. Everything around him had gone very still.

Instincts took over and his body went rigid, his chest hardly rising with breath and then he heard it. A quiet, wet gurgle directly behind him. His mind screamed at him to run. His muscles bunched, coiled to sprint faster than the wind. *Go now! Now! NOW!*

With super-human effort Monkhouse fought back, crushing the feral panic raging in his head until he could think again. He couldn't outrun the nightmare lingering at his back. How could the Vix have walked up on him? *I only dozed off for a moment, didn't I? How did it get so close?*

There was only one answer and it brought a gallows grin to Monkhouse. The Vix had been there the whole time. It was Monkhouse who'd snuck up beside it, not the other way around. *Let's see Tate beat that.*

His grin disappeared at the sound of soft rustling further behind him. There was more than one Vix. How many he couldn't tell and wasn't going to risk turning his head to see.

He couldn't stand there all night hoping they'd move away and, in fact, his time was running out. At any moment Tate would be signaling to move on the camp. Even if Monkhouse stayed still, the noise of the alarmed mercs would trigger the Vix to attack. It would charge, slashing and ripping into the first thing it hit, which was him. He had to get out of the way.

Searching his surroundings, Monkhouse saw a tree, to his left, covered in dense ivy. *Safety.* He could hide in the ivy. All he had to do was move, silently, with a Vix only inches behind him.

To Monkhouse, every sound was frighteningly amplified, even the brush of grass against his rising boot sounded like a bull charging through a corn field. Every inch of movement demanded absolute control and before Monkhouse had gone two steps his body and mind were in a war of wills. The muscles in his legs, back and neck were bunching and cramping, screaming for release from the rigid tension he exacted on them.

With the Vix behind him, Monkhouse couldn't see what the thing was doing, if it sensed his movement, felt his body heat, or heard his breathing. Maybe it reaching for him. Any moment he'd feel the rotted squeeze of its fingers dig into his neck.

No! Shut up. He couldn't allow the pain, fear, or hopelessness to consume him. He squeezed the world he knew down to a needle sharp point of focus; *movement is stealth and stealth is life.*

Almost at the tree, relief in sight, his legs began to shake uncontrollably. Sweat ran down his face, stinging his eyes, but he wouldn't risk the added movement of wiping his face.

He gently pressed himself against the ivy, sinking further behind their leaves. The black silhouette of the Vix stood inert, blending easily among the inky shadows of the jungle. Monkhouse now understood how he'd missed seeing it and how close to having his face chewed off he'd come.

His back came against the unyielding trunk of the tree as the leaves of ivy closed around him. Almost as if the Vix knew it had lost their game of hide and seek, the thing turned away and took a shuffling step.

Monkhouse ignored the tickle of sweat on his ear as he watched the Vix, hoping it would soon leave. Annoyance quickly turned to confusion as the tickle of his ear moved to his cheek. And then to the corner of his mouth. Something was crawling on his face. His hand instinctively twitched to slap at the thing, but caught himself before making that fatal mistake.

Monkhouse couldn't see what it was and didn't want to know, but morbid curiosity leaked the clues into his mind, piecing together a mental image he didn't want to see. The could feel the thing's weight, the brush of stiff hair as its legs probed his face before moving. The span of its feet nearly covered the entire side of his face from his ear to his brow, his jaw and upper lip. He nearly whimpered out loud as coarse hairs brushed his cheek and the picture was complete. It was a spider. It was a damn big spider!

Monkhouse flew past reason, straight to the worst case scenario. It had to be a venomous spider, and he was right. He remembered the name, Phoneutria, from the orientation class about dangerous insects because it means 'murderess' and at the time he'd joked about reminding him of his ex-wife. The Brazilian Wandering Spider was deadly and, if startled, it was dangerously aggressive.

The muscles of Monkhouse's face threatened to twitch uncontrollably and he clutched at the thin vines criss-crossing the tree trunk involuntarily seeking to bleed off the mounting wave of tremors he felt coming.

SNAP!

Monkhouse had forgotten about the Vix, forgotten about stealth, and had broken off a handful of vines. He didn't have to guess if the Vix heard him. It was now standing in front of him.

Through the leaves, Monkhouse could see the Vix, facing sideways to him, lolling its head from side to side, waiting for another noise, or trying to sense if there was food close by.

The spider's leg found the corner of Monkhouse's mouth and tentatively tugged at his lip, exploring for a way into his mouth. A spontaneous gasp escaped Monkhouse before he could stop it and the Vix wheeled around to face him.

It slowly leaned forward until its face brushed the leaves, almost bumping Monkhouse's nose. He constricted his throat against the gag reflex as the stench of putrid meat hammered him. Only rotted sockets remained where its eyes had once been, but the Vix searched with other senses. It lingered and inch away, like it was daring Monkhouse to give himself away. The spider pulled back his lip.

The shuffling of a distant Vix distracted the one searching for him and it stood back, its corrupted senses probing the jungle around it. But Monkhouse was on the brittle edge of his limits and hysteria was winning against reason.

The spider seemed to sense a change in the thing it clung to. Monkhouse could feel the spider become agitated. It wanted to hide in its new found lair. Unseen in the bristles of hairs of the spider's feet were tiny claws and Monkhouse felt them scrape his teeth.

A low, quiet, guttural scream rolled up from the depths of his gut and whistled through his teeth. He knew the Vix would kill him in the next instant, but he didn't care anymore.

The Vix spun around, plunging its cadaverous hand into the ivy. Monkhouse felt his head rock back at the impact as the bony hand slammed into his face. The claw-like fingers gouged bloody creases as they snapped shut... and then they were gone.

Panting for air, Monkhouse opened his eyes in time to see the Vix shove something in its mouth.

In a fraction of a second, his mind whirled through confusion, fear and disbelief to understand what just happened and the answer blazed into his mind like a search light.

The Vix had grabbed the spider! He nearly laughed out loud, but something inside him barred his outburst and took over his body. For the rest of his life, Monkhouse would never be able to explain it, but something beyond his shredded mind possessed him to act. Before he knew what he was doing he pulled his combat knife, grabbed the Vix around the forehead with his free hand and drove the blade through its skull.

The thing sagged against his chest and he pulled the blade out. Releasing his grip, Monkhouse stepped back and the Vix crumpled to the ground.

13

DOUBLE CROSS

"Monkhouse, acknowledge!" hissed Tate's angry whisper over the radio. Without thinking, Monkhouse grabbed his radio and keyed it twice, signaling he was ready to go. Only then did Monkhouse realize he'd already been through two of the scariest moments of his life and now he was about to jump into another? But it was too late now. He was committed.

Four bursts of static came over his radio; Tate's signal to execute that plan.

Monkhouse sheathed his knife and brought up his AK-ACR. A few hurried steps and he was in the camp. Across the clearing, Tate silently appeared like a ghost from the edge of the jungle.

Nearing the closest tent, Tate pulled his knife and knelt. The tent wall silently parted under the wickedly sharp blade. The sleeping form didn't move until Tate snugged the barrel of his 1911 against the his head.

"Want to die?" was all Tate had to say to ensure the merc didn't fight back.

The merc remained still as Tate put away his knife then reached in and pulled the merc's assault rifle out of the tent.

"Hands over your head," ordered Tate in the man's ear.

The merc brought up his hands and Tate slipped zip-cuffs over his wrists and clinched them up. Grabbing the merc by the cuffs he pulled him out of the tent. He tossed the automatic pistol stashed under the man's pillow and took the knife off his belt. Then Tate sliced off a piece of the tent and stuffed it into the man's mouth.

He did all this on faith that Rosse and Monkhouse had captured their assigned targets. There'd been no sounds of struggle or alarm. He rolled his prisoner onto his belly with his arms above his head.

"Make a sound and I'll carve out your eyes," hissed Tate into the man's ear. It was important to keep his prisoner mentally off balance, and only a horrific threat would rattle in the merc's head long enough to buy Tate and his men a couple more minutes.

He left his prisoner laying in the dirt and moved to the next tent. The moment he drew his knife he was committed to action. His blade glided through the tent wall effortlessly. He parted the fabric, about to grab the merc, but the pillow was empty.

Looking up, Tate saw the man was sitting, with his back to him, assault rifle in his hands. That he hadn't raised the alarm told Tate the man wasn't sure if he'd heard something, or not.

The merc flinched, but instantly froze when he felt the Colt's barrel press against his jaw. Tate reached over the man's shoulder and too the rifle. The man let go with no resistance. Acting quickly, Tate bound and gagged the merc before he thought about fighting back. As he dragged him out of the tent Tate sighed, releasing his tension, as he heard bursts of static from his radio signaling that Rosse and Monkhouse had captured the other mercs.

The refueled campfire lit the resentful faces of the captured mercenaries, cuffed and sitting side by side, they glared at their captors.

Rosse and Monkhouse stood by with their rifles pointed away from the prisoners, in a low-ready position.

"What happened to you?" asked Rosse, noticing the bleeding gouges on Monkhouse's face.

"Remember yesterday," said Monkhouse, "when I was afraid to get shot?"

"Yeah."

"I'm over it."

Rosse puzzled for a moment, but shrugged his shoulders and let it go.

Tate recognized Hall among his new prisoners and knelt on one knee, in front of him. "Where's your man, Bowen?" asked Tate.

"You mean *Andy*?" he said sarcastically. "Considering my current situation," he motioned to his flex-cuffed hands, "he bailed on us."

"That explains why your boobytraps were disarmed," scoffed Tate. "Where is he?"

Hall leaned to the side and looked around Tate at the tangle of disconnected cables hanging from the uplink equipment. "The same place as the satellite. The guy's a traitor. Now I get why you left him behind on that mission."

Tate picked up a pebble and studied it for a moment before dropping it on the ground. "I didn't," he said, standing up.

Tate looked back at the uplink equipment and swore under his breath. "I'm guessing you guys air dropped off the coast and inserted using the waterways with a RHIB. How long before he gets back to where you tied off your boat?"

Hall tilted his head, calculating his answer. "Moving through the jungle at night?" said Hall. "Four, maybe five hours. Longer if there's Vix out there..."

"Count on it," interjected Monkhouse.

"Bastard!" said Tate, hanging his head in exasperation. "He screwed us both. He got my satellite and your boat."

"No, brother," chuckled Hall. "Just you. I still have my boat."

"What are you saying?" asked Tate.

"I ran ops with guys like Andy before. They all got the same psychotic vibe. So I disabled the boat. You know, just in case."

Tate smiled and rubbed his chin in thought. Then went to Hall's tent and returned with his pack. "Where's your map?" asked Tate.

"It's the small, black pocket on the chest," replied Hall.

Tate opened the pocket and took out the map. Unfolding it he clicked on his flashlight and studied. After a few moments he clicked off the flashlight. "Rosse, cut them loose," said Tate.

"What?" asked Rosse in disbelief.

"Where'd you get this?" questioned Tate, showing the map to Hall. "This shows classified military locations of camps, forts and airfields. Where'd that information come from?"

"Is that a serious question?" asked Hall.

Tate knew the answer Hall wasn't going to give him. The Ring. The more he discovered how far reaching The Ring was, the more he felt like David facing Goliath. Sabotaging The Ring's efforts was making a difference. The Grave Diggers had crippled their progress, but as The Ring's power spread out, diversified, Tate and his Grave Diggers would have less and less impact until they were nothing but an annoyance. Tate couldn't let that happen. He didn't how, not yet, but the Grave Diggers were about to step up their game.

"Never mind," said Tate.

Rosse hadn't moved, expecting an explanation until Tate gave him a withering glare. Grudgingly, Rosse pulled his knife and cut loose the mercs, who stayed sitting on the ground, unsure of Tate's intentions. Hall was the last one to be freed, and like the rest of them, didn't get up.

"Thanks," said Hall, rubbing the soreness from his wrists. "Not looking a gift horse in the mouth, but why cut us loose?"

"Because of that airfield," said Tate, pointing to the map. "As soon as Andy discovers you disabled your boat, he'll know he's a hunted man. Time is against him and he'll be desperate to put as much distance between you and him as possible."

Hall shook his head, seething at the irony. "He'll go for the airfield."

"One man can infiltrate that airfield without drawing attention," said Tate, "and probably stowaway on a cargo plane, but..."

"The chances of five men getting in," said Hall.

"Undetected," said Tate, "without drawing a lot of fire."

"That's why you cut us loose," said Hall, standing up. "We have zero chance of getting that satellite back. Looks like he's your problem now."

Tate walked over to Rosse and Monkhouse and flattened out the map in front of them.

"I'm going after the Andy," said Tate.

"You mean the satellite?" asked Monkhouse.

"That's what I meant," clipped Tate, in a tone that did not invite commentary. "The mercs'll pack up and leave. Stay with them to their boat just to make sure. Any questions?"

"Negative," said Rosse and Monkhouse.

Tracing his finger from the location of the merc's boat to the airfield, Tate did a rough calculation in his mind. "He's got more ground to cover than I do," said Tate. "I'll beat him there."

"Why don't you radio ahead and have some troops waiting for him?" asked Monkhouse.

"Once they get their hands on the satellite," said Tate, "we'll never see it again."

"Like that warehouse at the end of Raiders," said Monkhouse.

"What warehouse?" said Rosse.

"Raiders of the Lost Ark?" queried Monkhouse.

Rosse only shook his head in confusion.

"I give up," said Monkhouse.

Tate folded up the map and put it in his pocket. "I'll check in after I got it."

"Hey Top," said Rosse. "Sorry about earlier. Not cutting them loose when you first said."

Tate gave Rosse an appraising look and clapped him on the shoulder. "We're good. See you guys soon."

The eastern horizon was tinged with gold as the dark of night slowly faded in the pre-dawn light. Rising above a smattering of smaller buildings, the large, bay windows caught the first rays of light as they broke over the horizon. In front of the tower stretched a drab grey runway extending fifteen hundred feet in both directions.

The receding gloom revealed the large, hulking form of an ancient C-130 Hercules transport plane as it squatted off the end of the runway. Tucked under its huge port wing, a cloud of frenzied insects circled the work-lights of a maintenance truck. Two mechanics sipped their coffee as they dangled their feet off the landing gear housing, which dwarfed their truck.

"Hey Spud!" crackled the radio next to the mechanics. "I know you can hear me. I need a sitrep."

The two mechanics smiled at each other and leisurely took a drink from their steaming mugs.

"Okay," griped the radio, "I'm not taking the heat from Flight because the Herc isn't fixed."

One of the mechanics answered the radio while randomly banging a wrench on the landing gear's metal strut. "Don't threaten me, Tower Monkey," said the mechanic. "We've been busting our chops all night trying to get this crate airworthy. Tell Flight it's ready when it's ready."

"Come on, Spud," said Tower Monkey, "I can't tell him that."

Spud looked at the other mechanic who shrugged in agreement. "Yeah, okay," said Spud, looking at the checklist on the clipboard next to him. "I gotta few things left, then it's your bird."

Spud put down the radio and slid off the housing, dropping to the ground with practiced ease. "Bucket?" said Spud. "Do you have anything left on the critical list?"

The other mechanic came off the housing and stuck his head inside the truck. He leafed through a work-list before taking another drink of his coffee. "It's good enough," said Bucket.

"I don't want it good enough," said Spud, in a mocking voice. "I want it perfect."

"In that case it's perfect," smirked Bucket.

"Well, that's good enough," chuckled Spud.

Bucket started collecting the tools scattered on a drop cloth as Spud walked up the open ramp into the cargo bay. Capable of carrying three troop carriers, the current shipment of two, fully loaded, supply pallets hardly took up any room. Spud smoothed out a patch of tarp, covering the pallet, and set down his coffee mug, then gave each pallet a cursory check, making sure they were locked to the floor. Satisfied, he took his coffee, snapping off the overhead lights on the way down the ramp.

Forty yards away, Andy watched from the shadows of the jungle. His clothes were soaked with sweat from pushing himself to reach the airfield in a race against the sun. He glanced at the distant control tower and then the sky, considering his diminishing chances of moving before the airfield was in full light. The *clomp* of the mechanic's boots coming down the metal ramp drew Andy's attention. He gripped his assault rifle and the moment the mechanic disappeared around the opposite side of the plane Andy broke from cover and ran to the C-130.

Using his binoculars, Tate scanned the distant airfield hangers from the edge of the jungle. Through the open doors he could see two small, fixed wing planes. *This will be Andy's target.*

Tate caught movement from the corner of his eye and swiveled his binoculars in time to spot Andy reach the side of a C-130. *Are you kidding?* Andy slipped around the back of the aircraft and up the ramp.

At the top of the ramp Andy found the ramp control and turned the handle, but nothing happened. He left the control and moved into the cargo bay, past the supply pallets until he reached the short ladder leading up to the cockpit.

Tossing the backpack, holding the satellite, in the co-pilot seat Andy sat in the pilots seat. He sighed as he settled into the luxury of the worn, but cushioned black leather seat. His body was cut and battered from his headlong race through the jungle to reach the airfield before the mercenaries caught him. Now, in the cockpit, on a military airfield, they couldn't touch him. The only thing left was to get in the air. After that he'd arrange to hand off the satellite to his employers and collect his sizable bonus, undiluted by having to split it among his team.

Andy looked down from the port window, seeing only the front of mechanic's truck from under the wing. He assumed they were still packing up their stuff, unaware of his intrusion, not that it mattered. They weren't armed. He was.

He turned his attention to the flight controls which filled the front instrument panel, left console, center pedestal and overhead panel. The staggering array of dials, switches and buttons was a testament to the age of the plan. Even planes ten years old had more AI flight control systems, but the C-130 held a special place in Andy's heart. He'd flown them during his time smuggling for the blackmarket. Most of those weren't modern by any standard, but at least they'd had automated systems and a VR heads up display on the windscreen. *What museum did the Air Force steal this thing from?*

Andy performed the familiar sequence of prepping the plane for takeoff. He smiled as he activated the gas turbine compressor knowing the sounds of the four turbo prop engines spinning up would startle the mechanics.

Outside, the mechanics involuntarily jumped as the engine's huge turbines came to life with a scream.

"Tower, you moron!" yelled Spud. "Tell the pilot it's not ready to fly."

If there was any reply, Spud couldn't hear it over the turbines and realized the tower couldn't hear him. Spud grabbed a beefy wrench and gestured to the other mechanic that he was going inside the plane.

Andy was checking the fuel pressure gauges when he heard shouting from the cargo bay.

"Hey dickhead," yelled Spud as he started climbing the ladder to the cockpit. "Shut this bird down before I bury my wrench in your..."

Spud stopped as his head cleared the cockpit floor and saw Andy's gun barrel an inch from his nose.

"Hi there," said Andy.

"Uh, hey," said Spud.

"I'm gonna need this plane. Is that okay?" said Andy, tapping Spud's nose with his gun.

"Yeah, sure," said Spud. "Whatever you want."

"You're sure, now," said Andy. "I'm not being a, uh... What's that word? Don't you hate it when you can't remember a word?"

"An imposition?" suggested Spud.

"That's it! An imposition."

"No. It's all yours."

"Well," said Andy, "If you insist."

"I'm um, I'm gonna go now. Okay?" said Spud.

"That's probably for the best," said Andy.

Spud's head slowly lowered below the floor with his eyes fixed on the end of the gun barrel until it and Andy were out of sight. As soon as his feet touched the cargo deck, Spud sprinted for the ramp.

Humming to himself, Andy put down his rifle and returned to the pilot's seat. The turbines were at full power and he pressed a button on the overhead panel to start up engine number one.

He looked out the port window, as the four, fourteen foot long propeller blades on engine one quickly spun up to a blur.

"Nice guy," muttered Andy as he started the next engine.

Outside, the mechanic's truck trembled on its shocks as each of the turbo prop engines buffeted the vehicle with their prop wash.

Fighting the gusting wind, Spud strained to open the truck door and claw his way into the cab, quickly pulling in his leg before the door slammed shut.

Bucket looked at Spud with wide eyes, gripping the steering wheel in panic.

"Radio the tower," shouted Spud. "Tell him someone's stealing the plane."

"The radio got blown into the field," said Bucket, thumbing over his shoulder, "with everything else. Same's gonna happen to us if we don't get out of here right now!"

The truck rattled and squeaked as the front tires lifted off the ground and crashed back down. Bucket twisted the ignition key, starting the truck. He threw it in reverse and the truck launched backwards as he stomped on the gas. Propelled by the wind, Bucket fought to keep the truck from flipping over until he felt the truck respond to the steering wheel. Still rolling back, Bucket jammed the gears into drive and massed the gas pedal. Chunks of dirt and grass flew up as the truck fishtailed across the field to safety.

Spud watched as the C-130 lumbered onto the end of the runway. Sparks kicked up as the plane dragged the lowered ramp and, for an instant, he thought he caught sight of something disappearing inside the cargo bay, but then it was gone.

Humming to himself, with his hand resting on the engine throttle, Andy checked the status lights and saw the amber warning light that the loading ramp was still down. He flipped the switch and waited until the light went off.

High up in the control tower, Tower Monkey, aka Airmen Danny Trayberg, gaped at the action unfolding at the end of the air strip through his binoculars. As the C-130 turned onto the runway, Airmen Trayberg realized he, the air traffic controller, wasn't controlling anything.

"HERK zero two, four niner six, this is Tower Monk... this is Tower," said Trayberg. "You are not cleared for takeoff. Turn to taxiway and shut down your engines."

Airmen Trayberg hefted his powerful binoculars and watched for the C-130 to turn off the runway, but it didn't. He focused on the plane's multi-paned windscreen and saw the faint image of someone in the pilot's seat.

"HERK zero two, four niner six," said Trayberg. "I repeat, you are not cleared for..."

Airmen Trayberg's command came to a sputtering end as the pilot waved to him.

The thrumming pitch of the C-130's four engines rose to a roar as the plane rolled down the runway, quickly gaining speed and lifted into the sky.

Boots pounded on the stairway and the door to the control tower flew open as a red faced Spud charged in. "Stealing the plane," panted Spud.

Airmen Trayberg stared in disbelief as the C-130 shrunk to a dot and was lost from sight in the distance.

As the C-130 past eleven thousand feet, Andy put on an oxygen mask. The C-130 had a cruising ceiling of thirty thousand feet, but breathing above ten thousand feet began to get tricky. At fifteen thousand lack of oxygen got serious and above that you were on your way to, what was called 'the death zone'.

He turned to the oxygen regulator on the port console and saw the pressure gauge for the oxygen cylinder was at zero.

"Oops," said Andy and pushed the yoke forward, nosing the C-130 down. He pulled off the oxygen mask and watched the altimeter until he got below ten thousand feet, then leveled off.

"What kind of world do we live in," mused Andy, "where you can't steal a fully prepped plane?"

Suddenly, Andy felt the plane abruptly lurch, as if it had been tugged backwards. Warning lights came to life across the instrument panel as the air speed dropped and the plane began to shudder, buffeted by the wind. To Andy's surprise the cargo ramp had just opened on its own.

"What do you mean, no?" demanded Spud.

"Why should I take the heat for you?" accused Airmen Trayberg. "You guys lost the plane. You call it in."

"Maybe we could, you know, not report it," offered Bucket.

Spud and Airmen Trayberg looked at him incredulously until Bucket shrugged his shoulders apologetically.

"Forget about who lost it," said Spud. "How's it going to look when they find out you just stood up here, in your little nest, and watched thirty nine tons of Air Force property disappear into the sun set?"

"Sun rise," said Bucket. "The sun rises in the mor..."

"I know when the sun comes up!" snapped Spud. He turned back to Airmen Trayberg and jabbed his chest with his blunt finger. "The longer you wait, the harder it's going to be explaining this mess."

Airmen Trayberg looked out the window at the empty airfield then put on his radio headset. Sitting down in his chair he pulled himself up to the control console. He ran his finger down the frequency cheat-sheet taped above the radio controls until he found the number marked CAP (Combat Air Patrol).

Turning the knobs to the frequency he paused, his finger

hovering over the transmit button. His mouth had gone as dry as chalk. Under the withering stare of Spud, Airmen Trayberg sipped from his glass of water with a shaky hand.

The transmit button lit up as Airmen Trayberg locked it down.

"This is Potter air traffic control transmitting in the blind guard, requesting combat air patrol," said Trayberg. After a few seconds he was about to repeat his transmission when a voice broke the empty static.

"Potter ATC," said a professional, female voice, "this is Roughhouse one one seven, over."

Spud grinned at the sound of the female pilots voice knowing it would double Trayberg's embarrassment.

Tenson ratcheted up Airmen Trayberg's spine as he prepared to reveal to the world, more accurately everyone in the Air Force listening into this conversation what had just happened.

"Roughhouse one one seven, Potter ATC," said Trayberg. "I'm reporting an unauthorized aircraft. Requesting CAP intercept and escort aircraft to Potter airfield."

"Potter ATC," said Roughhouse, "are you reporting an intruder?"

"Uh, negative, Roughhouse," said Trayberg. "Aircraft is United States Air Force, but uh, but left without authorization."

Static spilled from the radio for, what seemed a painfully long time to Airmen Trayberg.

"Potter ATC," said Roughhouse, slowly. "Are you saying someone stole one of your aircraft?"

Airmen Trayberg squeezed his eyes closed and took a deep breath. "Affirmative, Roughhouse."

"Potter ATC," said Roughhouse. "Authenticate."

The pilot asked for the authentication code, proving someone hadn't hacked into a military frequency and was messing around.

Airmen Trayberg slowly read out his authentication code and waited for Roughhouse to reply, hoping his earphones didn't fill with laughter.

"Potter ATC, Roughhouse one one seven," chuckled Roughhouse. "I authenticate. Vector me to your lost dog."

Looking at his radar scope, Airmen Trayberg looked for the

transponder signal sent from the C-130. Every aircraft automatically sent a signal allowing for radar to identify and track it.

"Roughhouse one one seven, track north," said Trayberg, explaining the C-130 was north bound. "Aircraft ident is HERK zero two, four niner six. The pilot is not responding on any frequency."

14

THE PAST

Thirty thousand feet above the northern coast of Colombia, Roughhouse one one seven snapped her F-15 Eagle into a turn that made her stomach sink and her face smile. To the uninitiated, they'd be reaching for the barf-bag, but to her it was the payoff for years of busting her butt to be one of the select few qualified to be a fighter pilot.

The F-15 was old enough to be considered a 'classic'. A respectful way of saying outdated, but nobody said that around Roughhouse. She'd proven what her F-15 could do in mock dogfights against modern fighters.

She switched her radio settings to the command frequency used by Mad Eye, her home base air traffic controller.

"Mad Eye, Roughhouse one one seven," said Roughhouse. "Did you catch that call about the unauthorized flight?"

"Roughhouse one one seven, Mad Eye. Affirm," said Mad Eye. "You are authorized to investigate."

Roughhouse grinned under her oxygen mask. *Finally! Something to do.* Flying air patrol got boring fast. To break the monotony, Roughhouse would play Trivial Pursuit, or Battleship with Mad Eye, who was annoyingly good at that game. The thought reminded her it was her turn. She looked down at the grid-paper of their current game of

Battleship. She was sure she knew where Mad Eye's remaining ship was, ensuring a rare win, but she'd happily forfeit for the chance to let her F-15 do what it did best, intercept and kill.

"Tally ho!" said Roughhouse.

"Try not to break that ol' school bus," teased Mad Eye.

"Let's see a school bus do this," said Roughhouse and pushed the throttles up on the twin turbofan engines. Capable of two and a half times the speed of sound, the jets launched the aircraft forward as if it had been standing still. She took small gasps of air to counter the sudden g-force that shoved her into her seat.

The C-130's cockpit shuddered from the turbulence of the open cargo ramp. It wasn't significant, but it would eat into fuel which was needed if Andy wanted to make his destination. He pressed the ramp control to close it, but the warming lights continued to blink.

He switched on the auto pilot and watched the altitude readings making sure it still worked and the old plane wouldn't nose dive without him at the controls. Andy stopped as he was about to climb down the short ladder to the cargo bay. Reaching over, he grabbed the backpack containing the satellite and slung it over his shoulder. *I worked too hard to let you out of my sight.*

Wind whipped and tugged at Andy's clothing as he stepped off the bottom of the ladder in the cargo bay. At the other end, the loading ramp lay open creating ten by nine foot open window into open air. Holding the airframe against the buffeting wind, Andy made his way towards the ramp control, but before he reached it, he saw wet splatters on the deck panel beneath the switch and realized it was hydraulic fluid.

He nodded in confirmation as he located the small hydraulic hose used by the ramp control. He wiped away the excess fluid on the open hose and smiled when he saw it had been cleanly cut. Andy turned around and chuckled as he saw Jack Tate leaning against the supply pallet.

"Really, Jack?" shouted Andy over the roar of the wind. "This is why I can't have nice things," said Andy.

Andy picked up the end of the severed hydraulic hose. "You wouldn't have any duct tape would you?"

Tate stared at Andy until his smile was diluted by the cold silence.

"You always were a buzzkill, Jack," said Andy. He slipped the pack off his shoulder and held it in front of him. "So, what? You humped all night through the jungle for this?"

"No. I'm here for you."

Andy's face dropped in momentary stunned silence then he burst out laughing. "Just you?" said Andy. His laughter didn't reach his eyes which flicked over Tate, taking note of what weapons he carried.

If Tate had his assault rifle, Andy didn't see it.

"Just me," answered Tate.

"Who was that I left all busted up and bleeding in the mud the other day? Oh, right." Andy waved his finger at Tate. "It was you, and by the way, have you looked in a mirror because, MAN, I did a number on your face."

Tate wordlessly pushed away from the supply pallet and headed towards Andy.

Andy tucked the backpack into a pocket of cargo netting hanging from the side of the airframe then closed the distance on Tate.

Neither man saw the F-15 Strike Eagle slip into position off the port wing. In the C-130's empty cockpit the radio crackled as Roughhouse demanded the big cargo plane turn around.

"Mad Eye, Roughhouse one one seven. They're not talking," said Roughhouse. "Executing a headbutt."

Roughhouse dipped her wing and slipped under the nosed of the C-130 then accelerated ahead. Once clear, she climbed five hundred feet in front of the cargo plane, leaving a wake of turbulence in the path of the C-130. Roughhouse banked and took up position off the port of the C-130. She slid in closer attempting to see through the glare of the cargo plane's windscreen and did a double take.

"There's nobody flying the plane!"

"Say again," prompted Mad Eye.

"The cockpit is empty," said Roughhouse.

Roughhouse banked away until she could see the entire plane and noticed the lowered cargo ramp. "I think the pilot might have bailed out. Mad Eye, if they maintain this course, can it threaten any military or civilian locations?"

There was a short pause as Mad Eye plotted the C-130's course on a map. "That's affirmative. Your current course intersects restricted air space for US Army base Merril, in uh, twenty minutes."

"Copy," replied Roughhouse. "Two zero minutes."

Roughhouse briefly slowed to let the C-130 pull ahead then slid behind and edged in closer. As the cargo bay came into view Roughhouse's jaw fell open in disbelief.

"Mad Eye," said Roughhouse. "I think I found the pilot. There's two guys beating the hell out of each other in the cargo hold of the plane."

"What?"

"I have a ring side seat. Both are in camos, but there's no identifying markings."

Roughhouse carefully closed the distance to the C-130. She could feel the stick tremble in her hand as the turbulence from the big cargo plane got stronger.

The instant he was in range, Tate swung, but Andy easily dodged out of the way. "If you came to finish the job," he chided, "you'll have to do better than that, Jackie boy."

"You always did talk too much," said Jack and stepped with a quick jab at Andy's head with a punch to his ribs. They both missed, Andy easily dancing out of the way.

Andy faked to the left, catching Tate off guard and landed three quick blows, the last one connecting with the side of Tate's head. Stars bloomed in front of his eyes as Tate staggered back and fell.

As he lay groggy on the floor, Andy casually removed a fire extinguisher from its mount. Hefting the steel cylinder, he pursed his lips while glanced up, mentally judging it's weight.

"This'll be messy," said Andy as he returned to Tate and raised the fire extinguisher over his head. The inside of the cargo bay dimmed and to his amazement Andy saw a fighter jet mere feet from the end of the ramp.

Andy walked up to the edge of the cargo deck and took a moment to appreciate the view. From this height he could see the gentle curve of the earth's horizon behind the sleek bulk of the fighter jet.

He waved at the pilot who gestured, in return, for Andy to turn the plane and follow.

"I'm a little busy right now," said Andy. He pointed to himself then mimed holding a phone. "I'll call you."

The pilot began go sign something, but Andy turned his back on the pilot and headed for Tate.

The F-15 banked away and was lost from sight as Andy reached Tate who was still on all fours.

Andy raised the fire extinguisher over his head ready to pulverize Jack's skull, but paused. "Come on, Jack. You don't have to pretend for your friends. Tell the truth. You're the one that shot me."

In answer Tate snapped a low kick to Andy's leg, smashing muscle against bone and sending Andy staggering back. The extinguisher clanged to the floor, and rolled away.

"You're damned right I did," said Tate getting to his feet. "You were selling our drone command codes to the Russians." Tate slashed out with a crescent kick aimed at Andy's ribs, but the younger man slipped outside the blow, catching Tate's raised leg under his arm.

Tate grunted as he tried to counter, but Andy was already in motion, driving his elbow down onto Tate's thigh like a blunt spear.

"Wrong," corrected Andy. "I was *going* to sell them to the Syrians until you shot me. But leaving me for dead and swapping the codes with fake ones? Talk about adding insult to injury."

Gasping in pain, Tate wrenched his leg free, trying to escape another attack, but Andy quickly pivoted under Tate's leg and swept his supporting foot out from under him. With nothing to grab, Tate smacked hard on the unforgiving steel deck, the impact crushing the air from his lungs.

"The CIA knew you were a traitor," said Tate trying to suck in air, "They put you on my team and gave me a mission to dump your body with false intel."

. . .

"Mad Eye," said Roughhouse as she took up position along side the C-130. "The pilot's refusing to comply."

"Did you make visual contact with the pilot?" asked Mad Eye.

"I was practically touching him with my nose," said Roughhouse.

"And he refused?"

"Not really," confessed Roughhouse. "He said he'd call me back."

"He stood you up?" laughed Mad Eye.

"These blind dates never work out," said Roughhouse, going along with the joke. "Please advise."

"The guy's a loser," chuckled Mad Eye. "Move on to the next man."

"Story of my life," quipped Roughhouse. "Seriously, I have a unauthorized flight and the pilot's refusing my orders."

Roughhouse looked out the canopy of her fighter, waiting for instructions. She'd have given a month's pay to know the story behind what was going on in that C-130.

The crackle of her radio got her attention. She knew something serious was happening by the flat, measured voice of her tower control.

"Roughhouse one one seven, Mad Eye."

"Made Eye, Roughhouse one one seven. I copy," said Roughhouse.

"Can you confirm the following?" said Mad Eye. "You have visual on Herk zero two, four niner six. Aircraft flight is unauthorized. Pilot has refused your instructions. Unauthorized aircraft is nearing restricted air space."

Roughhouse ticked off the list in her head, matching it to Mad Eye's account. "Affirmative, on all counts."

The pause before Mad Eye spoke was barely perceptible, but there was a sense of significance to it.

"Per the Commander of the North American Defense Command, you are authorized to execute rules of engagement," said Mad Eye.

"Holy crap," muttered Roughhouse to herself.

"Herk zero two, four niner six," continued Mad Eye, "is considered a hostile bandit. You are to engage and shoot down. Copy?"

"Uh, yeah," said Roughhouse. "I mean, Roughhouse one one seven copies."

"Good hunting," said Mad Eye.

"Tally ho!" said Roughhouse as she banked away from the C-130 in a wide circle. She wanted a safe distance between her and the inventible hail of debris about to fly off that C-130.

Tate lay wheezing, in pain, on the metal floor as Andy nimbly hopped back, giving him room to get up.

"You left me to die. When you reported me KIA they wiped my away my life. Like I never existed," panted Andy. "I lost everything."

It was beginning to feel like their last fight and Tate still carried the cuts and bruises to remind him how that ended. *If I can keep him talking I can buy enough time to get my wind back.*

"So did I," said Tate."Wrong, again," scoffed Andy.

Tate rolled onto his hands and knees, but didn't see the kick until it was too late. Andy's boot slammed the side of Tate's head and he collapsed to the floor like a puppet with its strings cut.

Tate's world swam in and out of blackness as sounds and words swirled around him in a meaningless haze.

"Rise and shine, Jacky boy," said Andy, slapping Tate's face. Tate's eyes fluttered open and came into focus as Andy as he stood over him with his hands on his hips.

"Your kid died," quipped Andy. "Yeah, that sucks, but you still had a great wife, whew she was hot!"

Andy glanced at the open cargo bay then back at Tate and got an idea.

"You had a career," said Andy and bent down rolling Tate over, towards the open ramp. "You had family, loyal friends," said Andy, rolling Tate over again.

Andy grunted as Tate feebly resisted being turned over, but it only took a little more effort to roll Tate ever closer to the open cargo bay.

"You didn't lose that," said Andy. "You gave up. That's why you're down there and I'm up here. I don't just roll over, no pun intended. I take a hit and fight back." With another shove, the end of the ramp was only a foot away. Cool wind snapped and wailed around him.

Andy looked at the sweeping vista outside the cargo door, admiring the view. His eyebrow raised in confusion as he thought he saw a dot on the horizon. A sense of urgency began to tingle inside him and he turned his attention back to Tate.

"The mighty Jack Tiller gets hit," said Andy with a sigh, "and he gives up everything and runs away."

Andy gave a final push sending Tate towards the edge of the ramp. "I can't even look at you," said Andy, stepping back and watching in anticipation of Tate disappearing off the edge, plummeting thousands of feet to his death.

Tate's leg flopped off the ramp as his body tipped on the edge. The wind caught his leg, dragging him closer to the edge. Then all hell broke loose.

Andy froze as a jarring, loud sound like ripping air slashed by the plane. A stream of 20mm slugs shredded the number two engine, blowing off chunks of metal in a ball of flame.

The C-130 nosed over as the remaining three engines growled, struggling to level the plane.

Andy looked out the back of the plane and saw the distant form of the F-15. Swearing under his breath, he ran for the ladder and scrambled into the cockpit.

Tate's limp body slid off the ramp, jolting to a stop as his left hand closed onto the last traction rung at the lip of the ramp.

Dazed, Tate looked down at the misty jungle canopy far below with numb realization. He looked curiously at his left hand locked onto the rung. His hand seemed to be acting of its own will. Tate wasn't afraid to fall, in fact, as he pondered it, it felt like he wanted to. He looked at his hand and tried to pierce his groggy mind, telling his hand to open, but it wouldn't. *Please. Just open.*

As the wind whistled around him he heard a distant sound. A sound he knew. He closed his eyes and concentrated. The wind dropped to a hush and the sound of giggling filled his mind. His daughter's face was alight with giggling laughter as the world around them whirled by. He was holding her hands, spinning her round and round as her body flew above the grass. Her young, green eyes crinkled with glee as she looked Tate straight in the eyes. "Don't let go, daddy," she said.

"I won't, honey," laughed Tate. "I promise."

The wind bucked hard, yanking Tate's arm, snapping him harshly into reality. His face was streaked with tears, but he continued to laugh.

Breathlessly, Andy threw himself into the pilot's seat as warning buzzers screeched at him. He grabbed the number two throttle and pulled it back then switched off the fuel pump.

He stared out the window, biting his lip until, at last, the flames that sheathed the mangled engine died out.

"Don't do that again," sighed Andy as he leveled off the plane and sank back in the seat. He looked out the window checking that engines three and four were still okay. Satisfied his gaze dropped to the co-pilot's seat. It was empty. He'd forgotten the satellite.

"Let's see how you like," mumbled Andy as he grabbed his assault rifle. He slid down the short ladder into the cargo bay, and his stomach sank. The cargo pocket was empty.

"Oh son of a..." Andy stopped in disbelief when he saw Tate standing in the middle of the cargo bay, wearing the backpack.

"Damn it, Jack," yelled Andy aiming his rifle at Tate's chest. "Why aren't you dead?"

"I remembered a conversation from a long time ago," offered Jack.

Andy waited a moment then looked up from behind the gunsight. "And?"

"If you shoot the satellite it'll be worthless," offered Tate unperturbed.

"That's true," said Andy, and adjusted his aim at Tate's head.

Turbulence over the wrecked engine buffeted the plane, making impossible for Andy to control his aim at Tate's head.

"Didn't you say you didn't care about the satellite?" asked Andy eyeing the backpack. "I thought you were here for me."

"I had my priorities wrong," said Tate. "I'm better now."

"I'm happy for you," said Andy and unleashed a burst of fire from his rifle. The bumping aircraft threw off his aim and the bullets hissed past Tate's head. Swearing, Andy tossed the rifle aside and charged at Tate throwing a flurry of wild, angry punches. The deft skill and lethality Andy had used against a nearly defenseless Tate had been replaced with the flailing of blind emotion. Now it was Tate who found calm in the eye of chaos.

No matter where Andy tried to strike, Tate was there first, blocking, countering, frustrating each assault.

Changing tactics, Andy caught Tate by the throat, but Tate locked out his arm, preventing Andy from choking him. Each struggled to break the other's hold and gain the advantage.Hoping to break the stalemate, Tate wrapped his leg around Andy's, taking his balance. As they fell, Tate shifted his weight, putting Andy between him and the approaching steel deck of the plane. Tate drove into Andy, with his full weight, as they hit the floor, yet Andy held his grip on Tate's throat.

"I thought you got your priorities straight," grunted Andy.

"Satellite first," nodded Tate as he tried to get his forearm over Andy's throat. "Killing you, second."

The plane shuttered as the air around the C-130 was ripped apart by a swarm of 20mm shells. The number three engine erupted in scorching shockwave as the F-15 gun hit the engine fuel line. Spinning at over a thousand RPM, the number three propeller began to radically wobble on the fractured shaft. An instant later the eight hundred pound propeller sheered off, spinning into the thin side of the plane.

The thirty foot wide propeller sliced down the length of the fuselage like a skinning knife, peeling the aluminum skin off the airframe from ceiling to floor and wing to the tail.

.　.　.

"That's one tough bird," said Roughhouse. The F-15's gatling gun could fire a blistering four thousand rounds a minute, but the fighter plane's ammo supply was not infinite. After the last two attacks she only had enough for three, one second bursts. On top of that she was pushing the outside limits of her fuel. If she didn't head back to base she'd have to answer for needlessly ditching millions of dollars of Air Force property.

"Mad Eye, Roughhouse one one seven," said Roughhouse. "I'm *bingo* fuel and heading back to base."

"What about the bandit?"

"Just wrapping that up," said Roughhouse.

Both men forgot their battle as air blasted through the naked cargo bay, throwing them against the opposite side. Outside they saw the wing begin to scorch as flame and smoke swept over it. The big cargo plane shuddered and slewed in the air as it fought to stay up.

Tate released his grip and tried to push himself off Andy, but he couldn't budge. Andy held him fixed, ignoring the hell around them.

"Do you want to die?" yelled Tate over the howling wind.

"I'm already dead," screamed Andy. "Remember?"

Pulling with his might, Tate rolled Andy on top of him, then kicked up, sending Andy flying back. Freed, Tate sprang to his feet, desperately looking for a parachute. But there was only the twisted ribs of the airframe where the emergency chutes had been.

The C-130 danced in the F-15's heads up display. The onboard computer couldn't anticipate the cargo plane's unstable flight path as it tried to target it with the glowing, aiming reticle.

"Screw it," mumbled Roughhouse in frustration. Her depleted fuel now a major worry.

She took a best guess and pulled the trigger on her flight stick. Fire and smoke belched from her gatling gun as she emptied the ammo magazine, trying to walk the stream of shells into the C-130.

"Mad Eye, Roughhouse," she said. "I'm dry. Heading back to base." Roughhouse omitted her concern of a glide-landing with dead engines. "The bandit's sustained heavy damage and losing altitude. No way she'll stay up much longer."

"Copy, Roughhouse," said Mad Eye. "See you soon."

Roughhouse turned off her radio. "I sure hope so."

The floor under Tate's feet bucked painfully, sending vibrations up his body. Both men looked down in shock as a flurry of 20mm shells sliced along the belly of the plane beneath their feet, kicking up floor panels into the air. The wind snatched at tatters of the plane's skin, ripping them away in long strips.

Huge holes ripped open, leaving the men nothing but the aluminum airframe to stand on. Each stared down, momentarily fixated on pieces of wreckage falling to the jungle canopy far below. The cargo bay rocked and shuddered as if possessed. Loose floor plates rattled and skittered out the back of the plane. Anchor straps snapped like cracking whips as the supply pallets strained to break free.

The flaming number three engine exploded in a rain of shrapnel, throwing a chunk of twisted steel into the neighboring engine. At 230 RPM, the thin blades of the turbo fan shattered against the offending steel and the turbo blew in a catastrophic explosion.

Andy grabbed the rib of airframe as the plane took a sickening drop. Tate was momentarily weightless as the plane fell away. He glanced at the rear supply pallet as it strained against its remaining anchor strap, then thudded heavily onto the rollers as the plane suddenly climbed as the auto pilot struggled against the impossible challenge of staying aloft. Tate grabbed a beam overhead and swung down onto a remaining floor plate.

Behind them, black smoke boiled out, behind the remaining engine as friction superheated the gearbox, and torque assembly. The cooling system flash fried and metal screamed as it reached melting.

Andy's eyes flashed to the tomahawk, as Tate pulled it from his belt and staggered across the heaving floor towards Andy, gripping the cargo netting around the supply pallet.

"After the hell you put me through," yelled Andy, "is it too much to asked that I get to watch your face as we crash in a ball of flaming carnage?"

The C-130 nosed upwards and Andy flinched as Tate's tomahawk flashed.

"Yes," said Tate as he held on to the freed supply pallet. Andy blinked in confusion until he saw the cut anchor strap and the pallet began moving towards the ramp. He grabbed at Tate, but missed as the pallet rolled away.

Andy screamed incoherently and pulled his pistol. Losing control, he fired wildly at Tate, hitting nothing.

The pallet snagged at the edge of the ramp for just a second and Andy grabbed his opportunity, carefully aiming at Tate's chest. Grinning, he pulled the trigger. The hammer fell with a dull snap on his empty gun. The pallet tilted back and slipped into wide open nothing.

Tate looped his arm through the pallet strapping taking a moment to enjoy the amazing three hundred and sixty degree view of the world below him.

Except for the rush of wind, all was silent.

Tate glanced at the cargo parachute, attached to the top of the pallet and tightened his grip on the straps, anticipating the pop and sudden yank when it deployed, but nothing happened. Integrated with an altimeter, the chute was supposed to automatically deploy at a pre-programed height.

Worry began etching lines in Tate's face as stared at the inert parachute, for what seemed an eternity. The soft canopy of the jungle was beginning to take on alarming clarity as the pallet continued to drop.

What if Andy stole the plane before the chute had been programed? What if the it was damaged by the explosions?

Dread quickly creeped up Tate's spine that the chute wasn't going to open. He was a dead man.

"Oh shi..."

BANG! A pillar of fabric shot up, inches from Tate's face. He gasped in pain as his arm was brutally yanked as two big, beautiful chutes bloomed above him.

15

A GAMBLE

Tatters of clouds drifted across the broad expanse of the night sky giving a dream-like glow to the stars. Scrub and tall grass rustled as puffs of breeze toyed with random bits of leaves.

In the distance sat a weathered farmhouse. The sagging roof and aged wood creaked in weak complaint. Next to it stood its long time companions, a barn and silo.

If not for the night vision optics, the buildings would have been dark shapes in a landscape of shadows.

The NVOs painted the world in frosty shades of grey, revealing sharp details and depth.

A dark figure crouched low in the scrub as it scanned the old structures, a hundred meters away.

"Razor lead, this is Razor Three," whispered the black clad figure. "Nothing on thermal. No indication of infrared sensors."

"Copy," replied Razor Lead. "Target is the barn. Move."

Five shadows rose from scrub and grass and silently closed the distance to the barn. Each held a compact submachine gun snugged against their shoulders. The laser sight on their guns emitted a beam, only visible to them, but insured the weapons deadly accuracy.

The buildings were bordered with gravel, but the figures made little sound as they neared the rust streaked corrugated door.

The figures wordlessly lined up behind each other and paused.

"Razor One," said Razor Lead, "open it."

Razor One pushed the flimsy door out of the way, exposing a thick steel door. Next to it was a keyless lock sensor. Razor One opened a large pouch clipped to his belt and took out a small box, roughly the size of the lock sensor. He placed box over the sensor then took a flat screen monitor from the same pouch. Two sets of wave forms appeared on the monitor and, using the on-screen controls, Razor One started to align the wave forms.

Tate took a slow pull from his beer enjoying the sensation of sinking into his couch as the pain killers muted the throbbing of his dislocated shoulder. His book laid unopened, next to him, as he leisurely contemplated going to bed early. Halfway into another refreshing drink of his beer, his computer chimed.

He leaned over and pulled the laptop off the end-table, sliding it onto his thigh, and opened it up.

On the screen was an image of Nathan, or Tate thought it was until he started talking.

"How are you feeling?" he asked.

"How'd you open a video feed without... ah, never mind," said Tate. "I'm all right. They tell me it'll be a couple of months before I can use it, but that's not why we're talking, is it?"

"I wanted to share something with you," said Nathan.

"Did you break the satellite's encryption?" said Tate, sitting up.

"No. That's turning out to be harder than I expected."

"I got a lot of grief from Kaiden about giving that to you," said Tate.

"I get the sense she doesn't trust me," grinned Nathan.

"She's like that," said Tate. "She said she had a *resource* who could break the encryption, but wouldn't say who."

"You should watch this," said Nathan.

Before Tate could answer, another window opened on his screen. It showed a bare hallway, viewed from a raised position. Tate immediately recognized the hallway at Nathan's place from the time he and his team had rescued Nathan.

The door opened and five masked figures entered and moved down the hallway, looking down their gun's sights as they moved.

Adrenaline flushed through Tate as the watched the figures glide into Nathan's workshop.

"Nathan," said Tate, "where are you?"

"It's okay," said Nathan. "I was at another location when this happened."

Two of the figures broke from the group, and began checking other rooms. The rest of them began searching the room, clearly looking for any hidden spaces.

"Is Vulcan 4 safe?" asked Tate, fearing the worst.

"It's fine," said Nathan. "I've got a handful of safe houses. They come in pretty handy."

"Okay, I get it," said Tate, his nerves jittery, but relieved to hear the news. "Someone hit your barn. You could have just told me."

"Give it a second," said Nathan.

Tate watched as the two figures rejoined the team.

"Nothing," said one of them.

"It's not here," said another.

"We can set up, outside," said one. "Grab him when he shows up."

"And if he doesn't have the satellite with him, then what?"

"We can make him tell us where it is."

"No," said another.

Tate leaned forward. The audio wasn't good, but he thought he knew that voice. They stood with their back to the camera making it harder, still, to hear them.

"I know him," they continued. "He wouldn't talk. This mission's a bust."

The figure pulled off their mask and long, auburn hair spilled out. The rest of the team took off their hoods and slung their weapons, but Tate was locked onto the lone person with the auburn hair.

The assault team filed out and Nathan froze the video feed, capturing the last team member after they'd turned around.

"There it is," announced Nathan.

Thoughts tumbled and clashed as Tate sat dumbfounded. All he could do was sit there, staring at the frozen image of Kaiden.

THE END

Thank you for reading Grave Mistakes.
Your reviews help keep this series going. Please take a moment to leave a review.

ENJOY THIS FREE BOOK

Add this free prequel to your library!

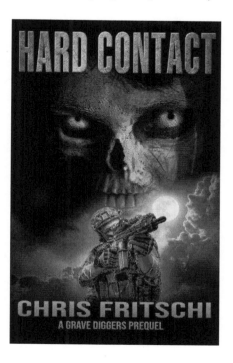

A simple mission turns into terrifying fight for survival.

This special forces team is about to walk into something more horrifying and relentless than they could ever imagine.

BOOKS IN THE SERIES

Is your Grave Diggers library complete?

The Grave Diggers

The Suicide King

Grave Mistakes

Deadly Relics

AUTHORS NOTE

Digging Into The Story

While reading this book you may have asked yourself, 'When did this happen? In the future, or is this a parallel world, or what?' You might (even) have gone back and reread some of it, thinking you missed the key sentence that explains it. To answer your (assumed) second question, no, this isn't a parallel world. In answer to your (equally assumed) first question the answer is *the near future*. I know. That doesn't exactly put a pin on a year, but if it's any help in narrowing down a date, you probably have enough time to work out your evacuation plan and stock up on MRE's before society is cannibalized by the undead.

I kept to current military gear because most equipment has a long service life before something new comes along. Look at the M14 rifle, for example. It first saw action in 1961 and is still in service 55 years later. I did cave to the temptation to come up with a fictitious weapon because, come on, it's cool.

One Last Thing

If you think you've seen all there is to the Vix in this book you'd be very mistaken. I've grown up on zombie lore and, like you, feel that once the monster has stepped out from behind the curtain you've seen it all. What kind of storyteller would I be if I did that to you? There's more to the Vix you haven't seen yet, and judging by how creeped out people got from reading the early copy of my next book, I think you'll enjoy it.

ABOUT THE AUTHOR

Chris grew up on George Romero, Rambo, Star Wars and Tom Clancy, a formula for a creating a seriously good range of science fiction, action, paranormal, and adventure novels.

Chris is currently working on The Grave Digger series, an action packed thrill ride that will have you hooked right up to the last page. It's Tom Clancy meets Dawn of the Dead and X-Files, and it's guaranteed to keep you on the edge of your seat. Jack Tate, ex-Delta operator, has assembled a rag-tag team of rookies and motley group of wannabes is all he has to go up against a secret cabal who are plotting a takeover of the United States. Can they do it before time runs out?

---

website: chrisfritschi.com